CORRIDA OF SIN

CORRIDA OF SIN

LYN WARLICK

CUTTING EDGE

ISBN-13: 978-1-954840-75-1

Published by
Cutting Edge Books
PO Box 8212
Calabasas, CA 91372
www.cuttingedgebooks.com

CHAPTER ONE

I T WAS DREADFULLY HOT in Chalupa.

Guy Moran stretched his tall, athletic six foot, two inch frame to its full length, and tried to relax. His angular hands hung limp on his flat abdomen, and Guy looked externally relaxed, but the back of his eyeballs hurt. It was fear, plain and simple fear, and inside him it was real. In about one and a half hours, Guy would take another step toward the top of his spectacular profession.

Guy was a bullfighter.

Each torero has a way in which he tries to relax before a fight. It never succeeds, but he continues to try. Guy's relaxation sat in the precise center of the ornate bed, in all her naked splendor.

Bambi, was hot in more ways than one.

Bambi looked exactly like what she was, a timeless human sex machine. She sat cross-legged, fanning herself with the corner of a white sheet. Stretching her long graceful legs, she eased her body from the bed, and stood in front of Guy. Even in a state of nakedness, Bambi was still beautiful; her breasts were high and firm, with artistically rouged nipples. Her thin waist only accented the sweep of her hips, which moved rhythmically toward Guy, passed him, and went to the window.

"Jesumaria," she waved her hand for a fan, "it must be a thousand degrees outside."

Guy raised himself, and crossed to stand behind her, his stomach touching and sticking to her back. The street was jammed with people.

"They're celebrating for the corrida," Bambi nodded.

Guy laughed, "I thought they were going to church."

"Silly," she turned and faced him, lifting her arms to circle his neck. "Kiss me."

And, he did, but it did not help the fear.

The corrida was set for five that afternoon, and the eighteen hundred seats in the Chalupa Plaza had been sold out for two weeks. Now people were dealing with the scalpers, because everyone wanted to see "El Oro"—the golden-haired American who fought bulls.

From the street, the noise of the crowd filled the hotel room, where Guy and Bambi lay side by side. His hand still rested on her hip, but her eyes were closed and her lips formed a contented smile. That was one of the things that Guy liked about Bambi; she was as dumb as Hell, but she was always grateful.

She opened her eyes when a knock clattered through the murky heat of their room. Guy playfully smacked her rear as she bounded for the bathroom, and her clothes.

Paco, his number two sword handler, came in with his Suit of Lights on a heavy wooden hanger. Paco had taken care of Guy's wardrobe since he began fighting, and he seemed to worry more about Guy's appearance, than he did himself. But, at a time like this, Paco could not be expected to understand how Guy felt. Guy was afraid. When it came this close to the fight, the prickling, burning sensation behind his eyes always started; not even Bambi could stop it.

Guy lit a cigarette, "Which suit did you bring?"

"The red one, maestro," Paco said.

"Good," Guy said. He liked to fight in red, it was his lucky color — the color of blood; a bull's blood, he hoped. While Paco worked, Guy went to the mirror and checked his face, rubbing his hand over the stubble of his beard. He had shaved right before Bambi came, and already it was growing again. Some toreros said it was fear that made their beard grow so fast. Guy agreed that it just might be. They all knew this fear.

Marcos, his manager, puffed in, sweat pouring from the sides of his face. "Caramba! It's hot as brimstone out there."

"Did you see the bulls?" Guy asked automatically.

"Yes," Marcos sank into Guy's chair, wiping his face. "They aren't too big, or too small. We got one with big horns, but they gave us a small one to make up for it. All in all, it's a fair lot."

"You look worried," Guy turned to him. "Something wrong?"

Marcos shrugged, "Nothing wrong, but there is a scout from Mexico City. They've been talking a lot about you. This may be a big break for us."

Guy chuckled, "Just give me a good bull, and I'll give him a good fight. Did you see Marge?"

Marcos winced at the name of Guy's wife. He wished she was not here, but he knew that she would be, damn her. "You ought to divorce her."

"That would make all the papers, wouldn't it?" Guy whirled. "You know she'd never give me a divorce. Marge likes money too much, besides, why divorce her?"

"She's expensive," Marcos pointed at him. "Damned expensive, if you want the truth."

"I'm not poor," Guy said, and added to himself: Now.

It was not something, which he could have always said, without it being a first class lie. Dear old Marge, he thought—when she come to his fights, Guy always had the feeling that she was cheering for the bull.

Not really; no one in his right mind cheered for the bull, unless the torero was a downright butcher. Guy certainly was not that; he killed well.

It was just a feeling Guy had about Marge; nothing he could put his finger on, but it was there. When he first discovered her little infidelities, he protested. He did more than protest, he threw the first one out on his can. Then there was a second, and a third, and Guy gave up. He tried to win her back, but it was a lost cause. Marge was like a hungry woman in a supermarket; she was ape for men.

Now, Guy took his wife's sex-hobby with a sophisticated nonchalance, just as he treated the fear that gripped him now.

"There is a reporter from an American paper outside," Marcos said. "You know how they are. Do you want to see him now?"

"No, not now," Guy said, "Tell him to come back after the fight, I'll be human then. They always want a handsome torero, and I'm not handsome before a fight."

The American reporters were the worst.

Marcos shrugged, and nodded for Paco to start dressing Guy, as a now-dressed Bambi wiggled through the bathroom door. She did justice to the dress, just as the dress did justice to her, and in the right places. Bambi was just one of a long sexy line in Guy's life. She came with him from Mexico City, where she first developed a crush on Guy. She developed it, until now, she was adeptly taking Marge's place in Guy's bed; there was nothing sentimental between them, and Bambi could not have coped with genuine sentiment anyway. She liked it on a sexual basis; that was more in her line, and she was good at that. Bambi had liked sex from the time she discovered that it was *the* game to play with boys. And, it was a matter of finance for Guy as well as a matter of sex. He was good to Bambi, and one of his goodies was unseasonably draped over her shoulders now, in the form of a platinum mink.

"Guee-e-e!" She could never get the American pronunciation of his name right. "I want to *keess* jou for luck." She lifted her arms, coming toward him, disregarding the fact that he was standing in the room, absolutely naked. Bambi was used to naked men; she spent most of her time with them.

She pressed her body to him, pecking with her full red lips at Guy's cheek and mouth. She felt good and soft, and pliant. Paco shifted uneasily from one foot to the other, watching the ritual of Bambi's version of *buena suerte*. It reminded Paco more of a bitch in heat, than it did of Lady Luck.

Guy held her tightly, welcoming her distraction. She was a beautiful, useless, sweet smelling, expensive distraction, and he needed her. He lowered his lips to the line of her throat, and the rich scent of perfume tickled his nostrils, as he pecked at the soft flesh. With the tip of his tongue, he flicked her ear until she giggled, twisting in his arms.

"Guee-ee!" She squealed, "Paco is a virgin."

Guy chuckled and turned to his swordhandler, "Is that right, Paco?"

Paco blushed and lowered his eyes, as Bambi filled the room with light laughter. Paco smiled, and Guy welcomed the relief of their laughter.

"It is time, maestro," Paco nodded to the immaculate Suit of Lights, and Guy glanced at the clock. Three forty-five. He turned to Bambi, "Another kiss for good luck?"

She threw her arms around him, and because what they shared was not spiritual, only physical, she hung on too long. She clung to him, and it brought back everything which had slipped away, with her first embrace. It all came back, the fear shot back through his body and gripped at his guts. She whisked out of the room, and Paco brought him some light lunch. A piece of steak, some fresh fruit, and a cup of strong coffee.

He was not hungry, but he ate, because he knew that the next few hours would drain him physically and emotionally. Marcos came back, having put off the reporter until after the fight with an invitation to the celebration in the hotel that night. They studiously avoided any mention of Marge as Guy dressed.

First the tall silk stockings, then the tight trousers that ended below his knees with heavy macho tassels. His white shirt was freshly laundered and stiff ruffles covered the front of it. He wore a long thin, black tie, and finished knotting it, as Marcos secured the artificial pigtail in the back of his hair. Marcos checked the macho tassels, to make sure that they were not too tight, or too loose, and made a quick check of Guy's trousers. A loose fold of satin could kill a torero. There were none.

They were almost ready, and outside Guy could hear the sounds coming from the people already in the plaza ring. He asked that Marcos and Paco leave the room, and then he crossed to the bureau, where he bad the only religious symbol in his life.

It was a small, exquisite statue of the Virgin of Bullfighters, La Macarena. He stood quietly, looking down at the small Virgin, and it was more a request, than a prayer. "Don't let them catch me today—give me luck, protect me once more from the bulls. Give me good bulls, and don't let them catch me."

Guy was now ready, as Paco and Marcos returned with Jose, Guy's number one swordhandler. Jose lifted the heavy, gold encrusted, red silk jacket, and came toward Guy. Jose, like all the others of Guy's caudrilla, was devoted to Guy. He knew his job, and this was the part of honor to Jose, placing the beautiful, gold and silk chaquetilla on Guy's arms and shoulders.

Paco brought the cape, a red one to match the Suit of Lights, with heavy embroidery covering the back in a massive arrangement of white roses with golden throats, and vibrant green leaves.

Guy folded it over his left arm, and he was as ready as he would ever be to fight the bulls. Marcos was at his side, as they crossed the hotel lobby to a waiting car, which would take them to the bull ring. Guy's three banderilleros and two picadors filled out the cuadrilla, but they had already gone ahead.

It was Marcos who saw Marge waiting at the car for them. She was stunning, and, for the benefit of the reporters and photographers, she gushed toward Guy.

It was something Guy could never accustom himself to; one woman in public, another when they were alone. There had been less and less of the latter, until in private they were almost strangers.

She was a tall woman, with ivory skin and coal black hair, which made her distinctive in any crowd; among a group of dark-skinned Mexicans, she was a standout, and she knew it. Now, she came toward Guy, her lips lifted to kiss him, but he brushed past them, and pressed his cheek to hers.

"My, my," she whispered in his ear, "Aren't you the modest one. How is your little buxom Bambi?"

"You're being nasty," Guy cracked, his lips barely moving beside her ear. "And where is you handsome Tacon?"

"He is scouting you, lover," Marge said stiffly, "He wants to meet you in a *mano a mano*."

Guy laughed softly, "He doesn't have to fight for you. I'll give you away. You're expensive, and he'd better be prepared."

"You're getting nasty," she leaned back from him, staring into his eyes with surface adoration. "I could make a scene."

"After this one? It would be anti-climatic." He grinned at her, lifting his hand, he touched his black, fuzzy montera. "See you at the fight."

"Good luck," she said.

"For whom?" Guy asked caustically, "Me or the bull?"

She patted his arm, "The bull doesn't pay my bills, dear."

"I'm handy," Guy agreed with her, and turned to the car. Marcos was waiting, fuming.

"What the hell did she come here for?" he grumbled and Guy shrugged.

"She said that Tacon wants a face to face match with me," he commented. "It might be the truth."

"For chrissake!" Marcos exploded. "He's no goddamn good. He's just pretty, and the bulls will make mincemeat out of him before he has time for a *mano a mano*. Who does he think he is, challenging you now?"

"Tacon," Guy said, "That is who he is, and he is my wife's lover." They fell silent, neither of them looking at the town of Chalupa as the car worked its way through the streets, mobbed with people on foot, headed toward the plaza. The car could not move fast, and a group of small boys spotted Guy, and began shouting, "El Oro! Oylee, el Oro!"

The crowd caught it, and turned to see the car, even clearing a small path so that the driver, Paco, could worm them closer and closer to the plaza.

The people shouted, lifting their arms and cascading confetti on the car. "Oylee! Arriba! El Oro!"

A cluster of girls at a corner squealed ecstatically as they rushed for the car. Guy like a matinee idol rolled up the windows with an electric power switch, but a mass of tiny roses was quicker, and they fell in Guy's lap. He picked them up and touched them to his lips. Then lowering the window, he tossed them back to the girl. She almost swooned, as she grabbed them and clutched them against her young breasts.

Women were putty in his hands.

He was their torero.

Guy waved back to them, and a new wave of enthusiasm swept over them. "El Oro!" They shouted, jumping up and down, waving, and as the car passed, they fell in line behind. They ran after him, their black hair bouncing in the hot summer air, their lips spread in a wide smile. "Oro! Oro! Arriba El Oro!"

Guy watched them, and smiled. They were his fans, his people, and they loved him. He liked it, and he was honest enough to admit it. All his life, Guy had wanted people to like him, but it never happened, until he became an idol. Now, they loved him.

"Arriba!"

"Oylee! Oylee!"

They shouted and shrilled, their voices echoing from adobe wall to adobe wall, and filling the dusty street. The car moved steadily, slowly toward the plaza, and at last, Paco stopped them.

Marcos went ahead, pushing through the crowd to the back of the ring. Guy followed, worming his way through the tightly packed bodies of his fans. Then at last, he was inside, and there were only a few friends. He stopped and talked to them. Some of his cuadrilla had gone to the chapel to pray, but Guy held back for a final cigarette. From over the walls of the ring he could hear the sounds of the festival, the trumpeted blare of pasodobles, the lilted laughs and voices of the people crowded into the bleachers, and the loud hawking of the beer and food vendors.

Where Guy was, it was silent. No one was laughing, because there was nothing to laugh about. The other fighter, a Mexican, shorter than Guy, came across the plaza toward him. He knew that they were not here today to see him, but to see Guy. He touched his montera in a salute, which Guy returned. They talked for a moment; finally he looked up at Guy, "Have you seen the bulls?"

His name was Ornega, and he was several years older than Guy's twenty-five years. Chalupas was a step up for Guy, but it was a step backward for Ornega. He did not have what it took, to go to the top and stay there.

Ornega shook his head, "They are monsters, big, black San Mateo monsters."

Guy nodded. He knew that the ring owner had bought San Mateos. This was a big fight for Chalupa, and San Mateos were expensive bulls. He had probably bought the culled bulls, which could still be billed as San Mateos, the fiercest bulls in Mexico.

There were four bulls, and two toreros.

Most of them would die today.

CHAPTER TWO

THE CONSTABLE, a withered old man wearing a wide brimmed black hat, mounted his horse and turned to Guy and Ornega. "Are you ready?"

It was four fifty-eight.

Both Ornega and Guy nodded to the constable.

He grunted and pulled down his hat, "We might as well get this thing started." He lifted his hand as a signal, and the parade began.

In front were two alguaciles in elaborate costumes, and as the gates flew open, the crowd roared to its feet, cheering in anticipation.

The band clashed into the song, *La Macarena,* as the parade stepped out into the bright sunlight. They crossed to the center of the yellow sand, each torero leading his cuadrilla. Behind Guy were his banderilleros, Pablo, Juan, and Chino; behind them on horseback were his picadors, Macon and Perez, their long, sharp lances held in the crooks of their arms.

"Oylee! Arriba!" The stands seemed to shout with one voice, "El Oro! El Oro!"

Guy did not acknowledge them. Instead, he walked stiff and straight, his eyes down, until they stood in front of the stand of El Presidente, the judge for this fight. He bowed slightly, then touched his montera and slid behind the fence.

Now, Guy turned to his fans.

They went wild as he lifted his montera to them, his arms straight up. He bowed back, and pasted a smile over his face. "El

Oro! El Oro!" The flowers came like rain, each woman aiming at his face, but Guy cleverly deflected them with his montera. "Oylee-e-e-e!" The cheer swelled over the crowd, hanging on and on, and on, and then picking up new speed, as Guy turned to another section of the ring.

"Viva el Oro!"

"Oylee-e-e-e-e!"

The air was split with the sound of a trumpet, and torile gates flew open. Silence settled over the crowd as the black bull roared out into the ring, stopped as the sunlight blinded him; hooked his horns right and left, little puffs of dry dust billowing under his belly as he pawed the sand.

He was a good bull, and the crowd saw it, and cheered it; not the bull, but the bull's good blood. Guy turned to Ornega, leaning against the wall fifteen yards from him. "Your bull, maestro."

It was a courtesy, because of Ornega's age.

Ornega was nervous, and his cape work was clumsy. His peon was a dullard, and too fat to still be in the ring. When he leapt the fence as Ornega came into the ring, the crowd roared with laughter, not at Ornega, but at the miserable peon. But it was disastrous to Ornega's fight.

In his prime, Ornega was good with the cape, but now he only made a few passes, and then requested the judge's permission to kill the bull.

He did, after three attempts.

Another gate clattered open, and two decorated drag-mules, with heavy harnesses, were led to the bull's body. Their work was quick, and the ring attendants swept the ring smooth and clean, just as the trumpet blared again, and a second time, the torile gates flew open.

Out came an enormous black monster, his head high, sniffing the air, and charging around the ring. Guy stepped behind the burladero, clutching his huge, cerise capote to his chest. He nodded to Pablo, his number one banderillero, "Let's see how he works."

Pablo, holding his capote, stepped into the ring. "Toro!" He shouted, flipping his capote in front of him. The big San Mateo stopped his prancing, and whirled at Pablo.

Pablo brought a charge, then a second, and all the while Guy's eyes were focused on the San Mateo's horns and neck.

Quickly, almost as if Guy had given him a signal, Pablo vaulted the fence, and Guy stepped into the ring. A cheer roared around him, but he did not hear it. He was watching the San Mateo, and the bull was watching him.

Holding his hands low, Guy let the water-stained satin sweep the yellow, hot sand. He lowered his head, but his eyes were lifted, staring at the black, wet eyes of the bull. The bull was watching the movement of Guy's capote.

"Torr-r-ro!" Guy twitched the cape, and the San Mateo lowered his head for a charge.

Guy brought the bull to his left, in a veronica, whirling the massive satin around, and the bull's horns skimmed within centimeters of his flat abdomen. He brought it back again, this time to his right, and the horn was so close that the crowd rose to its feet with an audible gasp, as the horn hooked a loose fringe of gold brocade. As if to show his contempt for the bull, Guy turned his back to the animal, and crossed slowly to the burladero where Marcos was waiting.

"He hooks to the right," Marcos said. "He's dangerous. Get it over with, the next one will be better."

Guy nodded to the stand, "They want more."

"They always want more," Marcos snapped, "Get this one over with, wait until the next one."

"I'll give them a little more," Guy said, stepping back from behind the burladero.

They were cheering, waving their arms, "Oylee! Oylee!"

The San Mateo was across the ring, like a huge huddled mass of bull flesh and black fury. Guy took his stance, and then realized that the bull was going to a querencia. He was hunting a spot in the ring from which he would not budge, no matter what Guy did. He had to do something to keep the bull on the charge, and quickly. A bull in querencia is deadly, because he will not come to the torero, and the torero must go to him.

"Toro! Toro!" Guy snapped, and the bull whirled at him. He whipped the capote. The bull lowered his head, bellowing as he roared at Guy. It was too dangerous to bring him in straight and to the left, if the bull hooked to the right, so Guy pulled him to the right. His hook would be into the air.

He wanted to get more out of the bull, and he forced the brute through two more veronicas, a natural to the right, and finally a Pass of Death that had the crowd on its feet screaming with one voice, as Guy brought the bull in closer and closer, drawing the huge animal toward him.

His voice was a low rumbled "O-o-o-ole-e-e-e," as he cited the bull, and wrapped him around himself, again and again and again, and the crowd went wild. This is what they had come to see. Again and again, Guy drew the bull toward him, the pointed horns getting closer and closer to flesh, and Guy wrapped the bull around his body again.

And again.

They cheered and shouted, jumping into the air, throwing pillows high up with their flying hats. "Oylee! Oro! Oylee!"

He brought the bull back again.

And again, and they screamed hysterically.

Then, he walked away from the bull, leaving the animal dazed in the center of the ring. Guy walked to the fence, and Paco handed him the big sword and muleta.

"Kill him quick," Marcos urged.

Guy nodded agreement. It was a bad bull, but he was Guy's bull, and now he was obeying every whip and whimsy of Guy's cape. He strode to the box of El Presidente; lifting his montera, he asked for routine permission to kill the black monster.

It was granted.

Holding his montera in his right hand, Guy circled below the stands. They cheered, the women waved, and he spotted Marge. She was sitting with Tacon, and Guy wondered what the ambitious novillero would have done with a bull who hooked dangerously to the right.

Marge smiled and waved, responding to the cheers of the crowd. She held her hands out, ready to catch his montera, when he walked past her deliberately.

She sank back into her seat, furious, as Guy tossed the black montera in Bambi's hands. She caught it with a squeal, lifting her trophy for the whole ring to see.

Then, Guy turned back to kill.

"Toro!" he grumbled, "Toro!"

The black monster grunted, digging his paws into the sand. The picadors had lanced him, and his head was lowered now. The first time Guy had seen a bullfight, it was the part of the horses which made him sick. Now he knew that the thrust of the lances was the only thing that equalized him and the brute he was facing.

"Toro."

He came at Guy like a roaring freight train, head on.

Guy planted his feet on the ground, drawing the bull close in with the small cape, then citing another charge. This time it was a Pass of Death which drew the bull's horns within a breath of his chest. He did it again, and then the crowd could stand no more...he swept the bull's head low with a derechazo, and in the middle of the pass, calmly looked up at the stands, while the bull's horns circled his waist.

They were on their feet cheering, waving their handkerchiefs for the judge to see, signalling their pleasure with Guy's performance.

Guy felt as if he were the only person alive, that he was standing in the center of the universe alone, now. He took his stance, spread the muleta with the sword, and in a low voice, called the bull.

"Toro! Toma, toro!"

And the bull charged.

Guy swept him past, and the crowd shrieked as the bull's horn ripped the red and gold on Guy's jacket. He ignored it, turning and calling the bull again.

"Toro! Ah-h-h-h, toro!"

He brought the bull in, his head low, his horns coming straight at Guy's belly. He held the bull in a true charge, the muleta drawing his head to the left, to avoid a right hook, and sword sank in, true and correct, plunging to its hilt exactly between the withers.

The bull staggered, trembled, and a low groaning bellow grumbled from its throat. Then it dropped in its tracks, dead.

They cheered and waved their white handkerchiefs until the judge awarded him the bull's ears, and still they cheered, and the judge awarded him the tail.

And, Guy stood right in the center of the world, and the world was at his feet.

He lifted the ears and tail to the crowded, circling the ring once, and then again, and they wanted more. He was almost thankful as the trumpet pealed and the torile gates opened for Ornega's second bull.

He was better this time than the first, but the crowd was too excited with Guy's work to cheer the tired little man, so he made quick work of the bull, muffing his kill again, but finally butchering the animal.

Guy was exhausted.

He sat on the bench, as Ornega fought, wishing that it was a three man bill so that he could have a little more time. He looked up, and Bambi waved. Then he looked at the seat where he had seen Marge and Tacon. They were gone. In El Presidente's box, the round, sweating scout was smiling and talking cordially to the dried up old man, who was serving as judge today.

It all looked good.

Guy saw that Ornega was crushed by the way the fight was going. He walked up to the old man, "You are a good fighter, maestro."

Ornega grinned up at him, "Gracias, Oro, but I am tired and old and it is time for me to leave the fight."

"Take care, maestro." Guy gave him a comrade's slap on the shoulder, as the trumpet sounded for his last bull.

Guy had returned to the fence, where Marcos leaned toward him, his arms resting on the fence rail. They watched the torile gates open, and the last bull charged out. The shadows were already creeping over the ring, darkening it, even as the bull charged at the first banderillero. A second peon went in, brought the bull to the side where Guy stood, and cited a charge. It was a small San Mateo, but with perfect horns, and an honest, straight charge. It was a good bull.

"You can't beat your first fight," Marcos said. "Do this one quickly; it's getting late."

"I will give them what they came for," Guy said, tapping his montera, and handing it to Marcos. "It is a good bull, and brave."

Running to the center of the ring, Guy knelt down and swirled the cape in front of him. The crowd was on its feet, but they were not yelling, as bull charged in and Guy flipped the cape over his shoulder.

He did it again.

And again. He tantalized the animal into a rage, and in the third charge, it leapt off its feet as the cape circled over Guy's shoulder.

"Oylee-e-e! Arriba!" The crowd shouted again. "Oylee-e! Oro!" It was like a roar, swelling from every throat, blending into one great shout, which filled the ring and brimmed out into the afternoon air.

"El Oro, oylee-e-e!"

Still on his knees, Guy brought it in again, and the sun caught the bright cerise of the capote, glittering like a lustrous jewel in the center of the ring.

The bull staggered, as Guy stood and brought him in a charge with a low, classic veronica, then a left, sweeping the bull closer and closer to his chest and abdomen at will.

Then the trumpets sounded for the picadors.

The black bull charged at the padded horses, lunging hard and straight, burying his horns to the hilt in the thick pad, as the picadors dug with their lances into his shoulders.

Once again, Guy brought the bull into a charge, as he knelt in the center of the ring. The bull zipped by him, and Guy pivoted and brought him back again, whirling the cape over his shoulder. He decided to put in his own banderillas. He took a pair from Pablo, letting the black head come in close before he pronged him perfectly at the withers. Two more times, he rammed the banderillas home, the bull's horns missing him by a hair each time.

The crowd had turned into a cheering riot, as Guy dedicated the bull and began to work with the muleta. He began with perfect derechazos, then falling to his knees he held the crowd breathless, as he brought the San Mateo in for a hair-raising series of passes, the bull grazed his chaquetilla with each pass and the women screaming louder with each charge.

The bull was exhausted, as was Guy, but Guy was in complete control of the animal now. He brought it in for three twisting turns, breaking its will, then stepped away from the dulled beast.

With a glint of mockery, Guy lifted his chin to a jaunty angle and strode to the brute. Leaning over from the waist, he kissed the exact tip of both horns.

They had never seen anything like it.

They worshipped him; shouting, they were on their feet, waving white flags of triumph, shrilling to the judge to award him a hoof—something which had only been done twice in the history of the Chalupa Plaza. The judge frowned, looking down in the ring, as Guy began to draw the bull in for the kill.

He killed with artistry, the only way he knew, and the bull had collapsed, dead, by the time its feet touched the ground. It was perfection.

Guy was king, as he circled 'round the ring again and again. He lifted his arms to them, answering their tribute with wide-armed salutes. He brought out his picadors and banderilleros, but they wanted only him. They began to throw flowers, the girls and women jerking them from their hair, and when there were no more flowers, they threw money. Pesos floated down into the ring, silver made puffs in the dry yellow sand, and his cuadrilla scampered, gathering the money.

Marcos caught his arm, and led him to the gate, and the crowd was still shouting, as he disappeared into the bowels of the under-ring, where the reporters were waiting. The scout from Mexico was surrounded, but when Guy appeared, they deserted him and mobbed Guy.

Marcos lifted his hand helplessly, "You are all invited to the celebration tonight. Hotel Juarez. We'll talk then."

Guy went ahead to the car, as Marcos hung back for a word with the scout. He was beaming as he got in. "They want you in Mexico."

Guy just nodded—slowly, slowly, his body began to be not afraid. The raw prickle at the back of his eyes stopped, and inside, the knots began to loosen. They hurried across the lobby and up to the room. The corridor was crowded with happy people, but Guy hurried past and into his room. Marcos left him, and when he was alone, he walked to the bureau. Holding his montera in his hand, he inclined his head to the tiny, beautiful Virgen de Marcarena.

"Thank you, Macarena," he whispered hoarsely. "They didn't catch me today. The toros didn't catch me today. Thank you, Macarena, thank you."

CHAPTER THREE

THE HOTEL BALLROOM was a mob scene, pure and simple. The town of Chalupa was still celebrating with firecrackers and songs. They were dancing in the street, and one man's name was the only name mentioned: El Oro, Guy Moran.

Guy collapsed after the fight. For a full hour, he stretched across the bed. Paco and Jose were the first to reach the room. They undressed him, and sponged down his body, massaging his tired, taut shoulders and arms, and gradually his legs began to feel as if they belonged to him again.

"You were magnificent, maestro," Paco said. "It was pure beauty, what you did to that last bull. So beautiful! Magnifico!"

"Where is Marcos?" Guy pushed himself up on one elbow. Both the swordhandlers laughed. Marcos was out getting drunk with the scout from Mexico. "You gave him a scare, maestro, with the second bull. He needs to get drunk for his nerves."

Guy laughed, and tossed them both a ten peso bill. "You need to get drunk too; do it on me." They started to leave but he called them back, "Did Tacon see the fight?"

"Tacon, maestro?" Both of them shrugged.

"Stop the game," Guy snapped angrily, "You know who he is. Tacon the novillero. He wants a *mano a mano*."

"With you, maestro?" Jose asked incredibly. "It's impossible."

"No," Guy shook his head, "It isn't impossible. Did he see the fight? He was with Senora Marge."

"Aiyee!" Paco slapped the side of his head, "Now I remember, but he was alone, maestro. He came to the ring during the last bull. A man like that'll never face you in a *mano a mano*."

Guy honestly did not know whether he wished they were right, or wrong. Tacon was showing promise; he had several good fights in the provinces, and that was the way to start. Guy had started in the provinces himself — the real honest-to-God hick provinces of a grubby West Texas ranch. His old man starved them to death by degrees, and the Mexican workers just hung on, when there was nothing left to hang on to. One of them, Alfredo Vasquez had tried his hand at bullfighting, but got out after his first gore. He was the one who first put it in the young kid's head to be a bullfighter. Guy's old man hit the ceiling, but then Guy was used to his old man sounding off regularly. He began to practice with a cloth and a calf, and finally he moved up to a larger calf, and a discarded capote, which he bought, with all the money he had, in a junk shop in El Paso.

The Army interrupted him, and brought Marge into his life. Pretty, saucy Marge, a San Antonio girl, who took one look at the lean, handsome soldier, and decided this was the man for her ... and, Guy was a peach-fuzzed virgin when it happened.

Marge was attending a rather exclusive school in San Antonio, run by rather exclusive nuns. They would have come unglued if they had known that pretty Marge Wipple had learned their convent habits, like a man planning to escape Leavenworth. Marge knew exactly when the last nun was tucked in bed, sound asleep. Eleven o'clock was early for a party girl, even in San Antonio, but it was beddy-bye for the nuns at Marge's haven of intellectual stimulation. She wanted something besides her intellect stimulated, and Guy did just that.

Even a girl in a convent school knows the facts of life, and the one sure way to latch onto a guy's affections. If the dessert is just right, he will always come back for seconds, or even thirds and fourths—all depending on whether he's a glutton for punishment.

The punishment, of course, was like being beaten to death with a featherduster, and Guy liked it. He really liked it, and he got careless.

Spring nights are very warm in San Antonio, and the venerable city fathers look with righteous indignation on people who undress in city parks. Boys and girls just are not supposed to undress in San Antonio parks, that is all there is to it, but Guy forgot the rules.

It was late at night, and very hot. They took a bus up Broadway, to Breckenridge Park, just to escape the oppressive downtown heat. It was utterly amazing to Guy, who had grown up in dry-as-a-bone West Texas, how awful San Antonio heat could be; it was like having someone sit on your chest for hours and hours. At least, it was cooler in the Park, so Guy and Marge walked deep into its cool shadows. No one was supposed to be in the Park that late, so they had the place pretty much to themselves. There was an occasional groan of climactic passion from the bushes, but, other than that, things were relatively quiet.

Except inside Guy's brain. They had been skyrocketing toward a climax of some sort for weeks, and he wanted to do something about it tonight. It was perfectly obvious to Marge that the one thing Guy wanted most in the world was to see her in the position of being about to get loved. She was right.

Marge did not have any big moral wall to overcome. It was simply that she was afraid of cops and irate nuns. She was sort of intrigued with the idea of playing jacks in the sack with Guy, only he had no intention of laying out his microscopic Army pay for a cheap hotel room. He found an isolated spot of dark green grass, surrounded and perfumed by thick oleander bushes.

They sat down on the grass, and Guy put his arm around her and drew her close. Her eyes were dancing with excitement, and she was slightly flushed, and Guy felt the warmth of her breath on his cheek, as he kissed her.

It was a kiss with a calculated effect—an effect directly related to an atomic explosion. It almost turned into that, before Marge realized what was happening to her. Her arms snaked around him, and held them tight together. Guy could feel the soft warm cushion of her breasts pressed against his chest, and it set off a tingling sensation which started on the nape of his neck, and shivered down to the base of his tailbone. If he had not had ideas about sex at the time, he would have gotten them at that precise moment, when her lips opened and his tongue edged between them, flicking in a gentle caress inside her lips. He braved the enamel ridge of her teeth, and with a striking probe drove into the dark feminine recesses of her yielded mouth.

She met him, and their tongues touched tip to tip, and as if it were by some prearranged sex signal, they began a ritual of strokes and touches.

Then, suddenly, she flipped a switch, and pulled out of his arms. "Guy, I don't know—what if—"

He reached for her, and she did not stop him. She wanted it as much as he did, and now Guy felt a surge of confidence, as he pulled her toward him and eased her down into the soft, green grass carpet. He stretched out beside her, face to face, his knees touching her legs, his hand resting on her hip.

They kissed again, and this time Marge was the aggressor. She was Diana the huntress, as her tongue jabbed between his lips, staking a claim on the passions she aroused in him. Guy was more than willing to surrender to her aggressiveness, and while they kissed, he ran his hand over the front of her soft cotton blouse. It was stark white, and Guy remembered very, very clearly the rounded shape of her breasts, under the tight peasant ruffles. It was a very vivid memory.

Guy was surprised, when he realized how much Marge liked to feel his touch. She pulled his hand against her breast as low, throaty sounds came from her lips pressed against his cheek. Her tongue, still the aggressor, skimmed the curved ridge of his ear, and sent chillbumps over his body. She wanted him to touch her, and to keep touching her, and with a rhythm made of pure instinct, because Guy was not the most experienced male in the world, he began to knead the warm womanliness of her bosom.

Guy was startled by the softness of her breast, as he fondled her. But slowly he began to feel her stiffen to a hard peak, pressing against his sensitive palm.

"Touch me!" she writhed under his hands, "You don't know how good it is, Guy. It's like being on fire inside, and everytime you touch me, I get hotter and hott—"

The touching bit was all good and well, and it might have been enough for Guy at another time, in another place, with another girl, but that just was not the way things were happening. He wanted more, and though he had never stripped a girl, he was going to strip this one, here and now.

She was afraid they would get caught, as Guy made her sit up. "Be quiet," Guy said hoarsely, "If you keep talking we will get caught." He pulled her cotton blouse from her skirt and lifted it over her head. She held up her arms, crossing them over her breasts as if she were trying to hide—whether from Guy or not, he did not know. He stretched her back on the grass, and now he felt the stiff, bristling lace bra which still held her breasts prisoners.

His lips found hers again, and his hands began to explore more now. She was full, and startlingly beautiful to inexperienced Guy. Of course, he knew beauty when he saw it, but, well, at a time like this Guy was in no position to make an objective judgment about her merits. He looked down at the firm little ridge of her breasts, which swelled over the hard rim of her bra, and flicked his finger over it. She giggled, "Touch me; you can feel me through the lace — it's so good, Guy! Touch me!"

Maybe he could feel her through the lace, but that was not how Guy wanted to play the game. He did not know enough about sex to know that rules had been made a million years ago, and they were just doing what comes naturally to any red blooded American boy and girl.

Still, sometimes the most natural things are not legal. But law was the farthest thing from Guy's mind as he unhooked her bra, and for the first time stared at her naked breasts. They were just beautiful—at least, what they did to Guy was beautiful. He touched them gently, as if they might be cotton candy and just fold up under his fingers, but they did not, and he traced his finger up their swollen mass to the dark halo of her nipple.

He kissed it, and any resistance Marge could have worked up on the moment's notice exploded into a million sizzling sparks of sex-hungry passion.

She wanted him.

Marge was no dewy-eyed romantic, nor was she even a virgin, but Guy built a fire under her that had never been built before. She'd known that someday, some guy would come along and upset her cherry basket, not that she had much left in it, but she certainly did not expect it to be a soldier, and a private at that.

Still, when it happened, she knew that this was a book she wanted in her library—so, she did not resist as Guy went farther and farther, and finally they were lying nude next to each other, and there was just one more thing to do.

They did it.

How they did it! All the things that had been missing from Guy's life suddenly lost their status as luxury items and became vital essentials, very vital, and very essential. Things had reached the point of no return, when suddenly the sweet-smelling oleanders parted, and a not so sweet-smelling cop loomed over them.

"I guess you two know you're violating a Park rule." The cop was talking to Guy, but his eyes were more or less permanently attached to Marge.

It all went, as fast as it had come, and Guy was abruptly in an emotional vacuum. Marge was fast off the mark, and she had tricks which could startle even a San Antonio cop. There was one very neat solution for the situation; marriage. M-a-r-r-i-a-g-e. Guy listened and saw that the cop's sympathies were on her side. It was a trite old story, but, oh! so effective. Poor little girl, enticed from the confines of her convent school, and brought into the bushes by a sex-starved soldier, who would promise her anything to get her.

Before he realized the full implications of what was happening, Guy was the proud possessor of a one-way ticket on a non-stop railroad familiar to lots of American males. There are no sidings and no detours on this railroad, and it has just one destination, and it is not Grand Central, unless they have turned that into a pagan palace of matrimony in the last thirty minutes.

A "quickie" marriage can be arranged, even in historic old San Antonio, and it was. Guy went back to Fort Sam Houston a married man, with instructions to sign over his allotment to his lovely wife. Marge found a small apartment, and it might have been a paradise on earth, if they had not been restricted to a life in keeping with the high finance of a buck private.

It did not go very far, and Marge was sitting on a potential Bank of America. She did not hold out on Guy, but he was away from home so much of the time, and it did not hurt it for her to share it—at a profit of course, and she was careful about things like V.D. The financial side of their life improved considerably, and then Guy was discharged.

Guy's father was eternally drunk now; they buried him with a bottle of the best Scotch, instead of flowers, and Guy was the proud owner of a sandy, dry, oilless Texas ranch. There is nothing on earth lonelier than a Texas ranch with no oilwells — unless it is the rancher's wife, who has been used to the glitter and gilt of a rip-roaring place like San Antonio.

The only things on the ranch were a few scrubby half-breed cattle, and faithful old Vasquez the ex-bullfighter. He introduced Guy to a friend of his, Marcos, a torero manager without a torero. They were naturals for each other, and Marge thought it was an exciting idea — being the wife of a torero put her into a wide field of contact. Guy auctioned off the cattle and the rusty equipment, and took the highest offer for the land, which was just enough to put him in training in Mexico.

He was good, from the very beginning, and what he did not know about fighting he made up for with a complete indifference to the dangers of this very profitable occupation. It was not that Guy was fearless, he was not, but he knew how to control it, in fact he controlled all of his emotions. That was why he did not toss Marge out permanently, when he found out about her hobby.

Like every other man who is a bullfighter, Guy was two different men. He was Guy the handsome, the pleasant and witty American torero, and no girl was safe from his amorous advances, if she was within a radius of five miles — most of them liked it, most girls do, but when it is a very virile, popular torero, well, they *really* like it.

Then, there was Guy, the bullfighter, dressed in his elaborate Suit of Lights, which was so tight that every part and particle of his body was on public exposition, who was scared stiff inside. To stand in the center of a bullring, and incite a black, raging brute to charge at his body, took a helluva lot of guts. One famous torero said that his knees started shaking the minute he signed a contract, and did not stop until the end of the season. Guy understood exactly what he meant.

Sometimes, it took hours, after a particularly harrowing afternoon, to relax. Today had been good, however. The fans were on his side, and the bulls had been good. His technique was getting more and more polished, and now they wanted him in Mexico. There was no contract yet, but Marcos was out now with the scout, and at the very least, they were interested.

Guy stretched, went to the bathroom and took a hot shower, staying under the spray a good thirty minutes. When he was through, he briskly dried and shaved. When he returned to the room, Bambi had arrived and taken up her throne in the center of his bed. She was dressed, fully dressed; nonchalantly buffing her nail polish, as if making herself beautiful was the most important thing in the world. She looked up at Guy as he came from the shower with frank, but familiar admiration.

"We going to the party?" She asked.

"Unless you want to have a party here," Guy grinned, tossing his wet towel at her. She caught it, laughing, because laughter was about the most serious emotion in Bambi's life. "Guee-e! Jou make a joke."

"It's Y-O-U, you," Guy said leaning toward her, "not jou."

She tried, but it still came out, "jou," and they both fell across the bed laughing at her inability to conquer English, and their laughter turned into a kiss, and the kiss made even more graphic Guy's suggestion that they have a preliminary party, here and now.

CHAPTER FOUR

BAMBI BROKE THEIR KISS and pushed back from Guy, looking at his face as if she were trying to figure out the details of a French maze puzzle. He was handsome, and right now he was just perfect for Bambi. There was something about a man, freshly showered with his hair still wet, that excited her. Guy could see the flush of anticipation in Bambi's cheeks, and her sparkling eyes.

But it made him edgy for her to look at him this way.

"What the Hell you looking at me like that for?" He asked, snatching the towel and heaving it toward an empty chair.

"No reason," Bambi said quickly. After a fight, his temper was like high explosives sitting on a red hot furnace, and Bambi did not want him mad at her. It ruined the evening, when Guy was angry. "The bulls were bad today?"

"They were good," Guy said abruptly. "Maybe I'd better get dressed."

She lifted her hands to him, her arms outstretched, "Come here, Guee-e."

He turned, his anger quickly dead, as he saw her this way. Now, she was perfect. She was what he needed, and Guy crossed the room until he towered over her. Bambi lifted her arms and circled his body, pulling herself against him until her cheek rested on the naked flat abdomen. Guy stroked her hair. She was a senseless sex machine, that's all she was, he thought, and all she wanted from him was money and sex. He had both. She made soft cooing sounds as he stroked her head, and her hands crept to the small of his back. There had been fear in her eyes, during the flash of his anger, but now when she looked up, they were full of lust again.

"Love me, Guee-ee," she sighed, "Now."

He sank onto the mattress beside her, stretching her back, and leaning over until their lips met and held in an open, warm kiss. Her hands moved over his shoulder, and Guy felt her fingertips prickle the short hairs of his neck as she began to undulate her hips against him.

Edging his hands up her ribs, he found the soft fullness of her ample breasts, and heard her sigh. She loved for him to touch her breasts, and helped him as he stripped back her dress, and Guy saw that she was not wearing a bra. Bambi had been around a long time, and she knew that Guy would need her now. She was a good woman, who used her body like a doctor uses medicine.

Guy squeezed her breasts and saw the blue veins which covered them like fine Spanish lace turn darker, and his finger flicked her rouged nipple. She squealed, and flinging her arms around his neck, she jerked herself hard against him until her breath was a hot whisper in his ear.

"Guee-ee! Gue!" Bambi muttered, "Keep doing it to me! Don't stop, keep doing it. I love it. It's so good."

He slipped her dress over her hips, and took off the soft, cool halfslip until all she wore was a set of thin, sheer nylon panties. He edged his hand to the round, firm hip, and he began to dig into her flesh.

"That hurts." she whispered, pouting her lower lip, but Guy could see her eyes, begging him to go on, and on, and on. Bambi loved the thrill of sex with Guy. Because it was so easy for him, he had lost his hunger for common thrills. He wanted stimulation, and she needed the same heady thing.

He moved his fingers to the knee mound and then circling he began to edge up the warm soft flesh of her inner thigh. Up, and up he moved his hand.

Twisting her head, she threw herself back, arching her body to meet the maddening slow progress of his hand. She stroked his arm, urging him on and up, farther and farther. She swung her hips in a sensual arc, swooping to hurry his hand, and then she inched toward him.

Higher and higher, he moved up toward her.

Higher and Bambi's eyes closed except for a dark slit, which glittered like a black wound on her pale flesh. Her breath came in hard gasps, as he leaned over her and covered her breasts with his lips.

It was sheer beautiful passionate insanity.

It was the place to go to forget, because at a moment like this there was nothing which could come to break the hot excitement, except the hotter pounding of then blood.

Higher he moved his hand.

She groaned and writhed against him.

"Guee-e! Touch me!" She pleaded, jerking so that her body thrust closer to his hand.

Up, and the smooth skin of her inner thigh felt like rich luxurious velvet.

His nostrils flared, and Guy's own breath came in shorter and shorter gasps. The thought of taking her was his only idea, and it was seared in his brain like the brand on a bull.

The room was full of the heavy scent of her perfume, and her body felt like soft cushions as Guy leaned over her again, and she moved to make room for him with her legs. He buried his face in the warm sweetness of her breasts, and the perfume made him think of blooming desert flowers and open places— wide open places with no bulls.

She gave a cry of startled ecstasy as he came against her, with the same accuracy he used to pierce a bull's withers, only now the thrust did not kill. Instead, Bambi came to life as if a violent storm had taken possession of her. She thrust against him, driving harder and harder. She covered her breasts with his hands, and his fingers dug into her flesh harder and harder, clamping against her until the nipple stood peaked as though it would burst — like a bull's heart burst when he jabbed in the long, slender muleta.

But there was no ring, no shouting crowds. There was just him and her, and they were in a high place, a very high place, and the air was thinner. It was harder to breathe, and they were going up. And up. Up.

On and on. Up.

On.

Up.

Suddenly, she heaved against him, and a scream pierced her lips, as the whole world erupted between them.

Guy fell over her, trembling, exhausted.

Now, there were no bulls anywhere. There was no hot, dusty circle of yellow sand, stained with the butcher's laundry mark. There was no circle of hysterical women, waving their white handkerchiefs at an amazed judge. There was no scout from Mexico City.

There was only this soft, trembling woman against him.

She lay very still, very close, and for a long time, they clung to one another, still locked in the position of their passion.

Then, she moved against him. It was not much of a movement, but just enough to bring the reality in which they existed back into Guy's mind. But he was prepared for it now.

He stroked Bambi's face, his hand lingering on her cheek for a long time, "Thank you, Bambi."

She smiled softly, "Sometimes, I hate the bulls, but today I was proud. I like it today, the way you give me the bull. Give me a bull another time."

"Is a bull all you want?" He asked.

She giggled and twisted out of his arms, "Silly! I like money," and then she rolled against him, tilting her lips to his face. "I like you, like this. This is good with you. You make me think I'm crazy for just this."

Guy grinned playfully, "For just this?" He swatted her rear with a light smack, which made a lot more noise than it created pain. Still, Bambi knew that for her it was mission accomplished. She had done what was expected of her, and he was happy. As long as Guy was happy, Bambi's life orbited correctly. She did not love him, her relationship was professional, but Bambi took pride in what she did to Guy. She was the only person, at least as far as she knew, who could turn him from a taut, keyed-up torero to a laughing man. She was not always successful, but each time, she waited for him to laugh. His laugh started with a low rumble and then grew, and she joined in.

"Jou hit me!" She cried in mock anger.

"Y-o-u, not 'jou' but *you*," Guy corrected.

Bambi wrinkled her nose at him, and made an effort at concentrating on the American pronounciation of jou. Her tongue was not near so limber as her hips, and it still came out with a Mexican jou.

He grinned and cuffed her shoulder, "Get dressed, woman. There are reporters waiting for us, and can't you just see the headlines: 'Torero and Girl Friend Naked in Bed!' "

She laughed, "It would be awful to be in bed with all our clothes on. I bet even American reporters would like being naked best."

"Great Hannah, Bambi," Guy laughed. "Is that all you think about?"

"I'm good," she said, and this time she was right. Bambi was very good in bed, and very good for Guy. What she accomplished was obvious to Marcos, and pleasantly inobvious to the others, who greeted Guy as he came into the hotel ballroom.

It was large, and ornately Spanish in a heavy colonial way. Great polished wood beams crisscrossed the ceiling, and heavy chandeliers of hammered brass made a brave attempt to lighten the room. They failed, just as the inadequate air conditioning failed against the large puffs of gray cigar smoke that caused a low hanging cloud approximately four feet above Guy's head.

Marcos was the first to reach Guy, and with the astute judgment of an excellent manager, he hustled Bambi away from Guy's side. He was alone, when the first reporter faced him. It was a flat-faced man, who drank too much, but represented a news rag in the States. Guy was a novelty to him, like a Christmas tinsel ball. It would be a good space filler—and the reporter desperately needed something to reach the home office from his desk.

"Why are you, an American, in the bull fighting business?" He raised a rudely prying face to Guy, a dead cigar butt bounced in the corner of his mouth, and Guy had seen his kind before. He could almost read his mind: 'An American bum, cashing in on his good looks and making a play for publicity.' It had been printed before, and the first time, Guy got mad and slapped a law suit against the paper. The second time, it was easier to ignore, and by now it was the expected reaction.

"Why are you a newspaper reporter?" Guy returned his question.

"Senor Moran, will you accept the offer to fight in El Plaza de Toros?" a Mexican reporter interrupted them. Guy told him that he knew nothing of the offer, but that he would ask his manager.

The fat American reporter nudged closer, "Americans aren't usually in the bull fighting business. Is it for the money?"

Guy nodded, "That's a big part of it."

"Are you afraid?" He demanded, chomping on the cigar.

"Senor Moran," another Mexican pushed near Guy. "Do you like San Mateos?"

Guy grinned, shrugged, "If a man has to choose, a San Mateo is the best one to fight."

"Are you afraid?" The American repeated his question, pushing between Guy and the Mexican reporters.

Guy looked him in the face, and felt utter contempt for the softness he saw there. The reporter was a man who had never faced anything so dangerous as a charging bull. His greatest show of bravery was now as he tried to badger Guy into saying something which he would later regret. Guy nodded, "Have you ever known fear that gripped your guts, and tied you up in knots? Do you know what fear is like when it prickles the back of your eyeballs and burns in your head?"

"Then you are afraid," the reporter scribbled on a pad, without looking up.

"Every bullfighter is afraid of the bulls," Guy said. "Yes, I'm afraid. Every time I step into that ring, I'm afraid."

"Why do you stay in the ring?" Guy heard the question and saw the other reporters come to alert. It was a question he'd asked himself many times. Just why did he stay in the ring? Guy mulled it over. Part of it was the money; the ring paid well, especially now he was rising in the profession. Every time he was billed, the ticket vendors sold out days before the fight. Maybe there was some sort of subconscious desire to prove himself, but Guy was no psychologist. Still, he knew it was important. He needed excitement to live, and if fighting was taken from his life, it would be dull and drab. He was one of the people who substituted excitement for everything else that fills other people's lives—that was why he could go without things like a faithful wife.

Marge certainly was not faithful Guy saw her as he left the reporters and pushed his way toward his table. She was there, but so was glamourpuss Tacon, and Bambi was seated next to a vacant chair; his chair. Marcos was clever about it, placing Guy between Marge and Bambi, that way no one could say that El Oro was attached to either woman, and his fans would naturally presume that he was there beside his wife. Divorce could be an unsavory thing in Mexico, especially when a new fighter was going to the top. After he was there, it would not make so much difference, but for the time being it had to be a game of charades.

"Bienvenido, maestro," Tacon stood up as Guy came to the table. It was the correct greeting of a novillero to a full fledged fighter, but Tacon made it with just enough insolence to prove to Guy that he was serious about the *mano a mano* rumor, and Guy wondered just when the clever boy would make his move. Tacon gave him no hint.

"Kiss me, lover," Marge lifted her face to Guy. As he leaned over and touched her lips with his both their eyes were open and Guy thought he saw laughter in Marge's—at him or with him, he did not know. She broke their kiss and patted the vacant chair. "Here, what are you drinking these days?"

"Tequila with lemon," Guy told the waiter.

Marge laughed, "You've gone native!"

He felt Bambi's warm hand reach for his. He managed a laugh with Marge, "I just happen to be in the mood for tequila. I don't have a fight tomorrow, so I think I just might tie on a hellava drunk."

The waiter placed a small bowl of sliced lemon at his elbow, and a whiskey glass of clear tequila. Guy sprinkled salt on the ball of his hand, slipped a slice of lemon into his mouth, as Tacon lifted his glass to Guy.

"To the bulls, maestro."

"To the good bulls," Guy lifted his own glass, and Bambi touched hers with his, and Guy remembered that she had said she was afraid today. It caused him to look at her speculatively, wondering if dear Bambi was capable of genuine concern. Of course she was concerned, he snapped to himself. If he got bad bulls, he had bad fights, and Bambi liked good fights, because good fights brought more money, and more money meant that Bambi's security became even more secure, plus the fringe benefits increased.

Guy dropped his free hand to his leg, and felt Bambi's warm hand cover it. Her long graceful fingernails traced the tendons of his hand, and then she shifted in her chair. Guy was watching Marge and Tacon dance, as Bambi lifted his hand and rested it on her knee. When he glanced at her, she was smiling.

"Jou unhappy, Guee-e?" She leaned toward him, her perfume coming with a renewed impact. "Smile, Guee-e."

"Dance?" He asked.

She was on her feet quickly, "Bien." She lifted her arms to him, and again Guy noticed with interest the physical perfection of Bambi's graceful body. He led her to the crowded floor, pulling her tight against him. There was not room to dance apart, and Guy was glad. The encounter with Marge and Tacon had set the pace for the evening, and Guy wished to hell it was over. Unless something pretty spectacular happened, it was going to end with him on a razor edge, with a raw temper. When he was like that, he did not even like himself.

Bambi felt good in his arms, very soft and feminine. She pressed against him, until through the fabric of his coat and her dress, he could feel the cushion of her breasts. This time she was not wearing a bra, and he knew she had done it deliberately for his benefit. Reaching to the inside of his coat, his hand brushed the conical tip of her breast, nudging gently against him.

"Jou like?" She tilted her head, and beamed a smile.

Guy agreed, but he wondered if Bambi had any idea that a man did not take the same medicine for tuberculosis as he did for a headache. To Bambi, there was one cure-all remedy for everything; sex. The floor was growing more and more crowded, and the couples were pushing against them tighter. The band blared louder and brassier, and Bambi squeezed tighter against his hips, until Guy could not help but react to the undulation of her hips against him.

The music went on and on, and on, and Guy dropped his hand from Bambi's waist until his palm rested on the bulge of her hip. She liked it, when Guy pressed her even harder, and his fingers felt strong and demanding through the back of her dress.

"Jou like?"

"Of course, I'm human," Guy grinned.

"Very human, lover," Marge leaned toward him from Tacon's embrace, "And very imprudent."

"And what does Tacon do to you?" Guy asked caustically.

Marge's laughter was loud and metallic, "We play checkers, lover. Tacon is good; he jumps me practically every move."

"I bet," Guy turned Bambi so that his back was to Marge and deliberately made room for another couple to come between them.

With Bambi nuzzled against his shoulder, and his back to Marge, Guy had a chance to look over the room. All the people here came because of him. Marcos had started having these little parties to take care of everyone, and to make it easier for Guy, as he became more popular. There were people who had to be considered, such as the press. He saw the surly American reporter at the bar now, and dismissed him. The ones who counted, were the ones who could make or break a bullfighter, and even if the American reporter wrote a glowing story, there was not even an outside chance that Guy would be popular on the mainstreets of Kansas or Iowa.

The important places were Monterey, Agua Caliente and Mexico...even Juarez was more important than New York in Guy's business. The Mexican reporters were happy, crowded around the bar, but Guy's attention stopped on one particular reporter, a girl. She was tallish for a Mexican woman, and beautiful with glossy black hair and a perfect olive complexion. She leaned against the bar, and Guy spotted the shoulder strap photographer's bag resting on the stool beside her. She saw him watching her, and moved her lips as if to speak. Then she nodded toward the door leading into a private room.

When the music stopped, Guy walked Bambi back to the table, where Marge and Tacon were waiting. Marge belted a tall tequila, and it was obvious to Guy that this was not her first. "What room are you in?" she asked Guy. "I may want to come up and see my ever-lovin' husband."

"What's the matter, you running short of petty cash?" he asked, sitting down beside Bambi.

Marge leaned toward him, "Maybe it's not money I'm interested in. Maybe I've got ideas about you, and what I'm missing these days."

Guy sipped his tequila, and felt Bambi's hand return to his leg, "There's always Tacon."

Marge turned to the handsome novillero, "That's right. There's always Tacon, but remember lover, we're married—all legal like. Maybe I just want to talk to my husband."

"About what?"

"About Tacon, here," Marge waved to him and Tacon flashed Guy a smile. "You tell him, Tacon."

"How about a *man*—"

"I know what you want," Guy interrupted him, and Tacon showed obvious irritation. "You don't have to prove that you're a man to me, and you certainly shouldn't have to prove it to Marge. I'm not going to fight you for her, you're welcome to her; lock, stock and body."

"You bastard!" Marge hissed.

"Senor, I intend to fight you," Tacon said. "I want to meet you in the ring, face to face." He was on his feet now, leaning toward Guy. He was too young to have any control of himself now, so his face betrayed his anger. He was being deliberately infuriated, for Marge's sake. She might have been impressed, but Guy was amused.

"I don't make my own fights, Tacon," Guy said quietly, motioning for him to sit down and lower his voice before they started shouting at one another. Guy held his glass in his thumb and forefinger, circling it in the water-ring on the table. He waited until Tacon had calmed down, and under the table, he felt Bambi's hand resting tiredly on his leg. He reached under, lifted her hand, and placed it in her own lap. Leaning toward her, he whispered.

"Go to your room, Bambi. I want to talk business."

She wrinkled her nose, "With him?"

"With him," Guy nodded, "Now run."

"Jou crazy to let him talk to jou that way," Bambi stood up. "He's a baby."

They watched her leave, the motion of her hips, rolling with each step held both Guy and Tacon's eyes. If he had not known everything that moved and wiggled under Bambi's dress, she might have been even more of a challenge to Guy. When she was out of sight, Guy turned back to Tacon and Marge.

"Don't try for a *mano a mano,* Tacon," he said. "We both know that you could not do it, no matter what Marge tells you. Every trade demands an apprenticeship, and you've got a lot to learn. Maybe a year from now, you can talk to Marcos."

"I'll meet you now," Tacon said quickly, and Marge grinned at Guy as if to say, 'See, he dances my trick.'

"Not if I have anything to say about it," Marcos walked up behind Tacon, and took Bambi's empty chair. Then, as if Marge and Tacon never existed, he turned to Guy. "Can we talk alone?"

"We'll leave," Marge stood up, pulling Tacon's hand. "Just don't forget, lover, I may come see you tonight."

"Don't count on my being there," Guy said.

Marge shrugged, "I know which is Bambi's room also."

Marcos watched her leave, doing a slow burn. "I dislike that bitch more everytime I see her. You ought to divorce her, if—"

"What did you want to see me about?" Guy asked. "I've got something I want to do."

"What?" Marcos opened his eyes wide, "Or should I say, who?"

"You wanted to talk?" Guy reminded his manager. "So, talk."

"It's about Don Juan San Benito." Guy whistled at Marcos' mention of one of the biggest names in Mexican bullfighting. Don Juan was not a fighter. Even better, he was the owner of one of the largest ganaderias in Mexico. It was a place where they raised the fighting bulls, and a profession which was so highly respected that the breeders were viewed as if they were kings or something. Not everyone could raise a good fighting bull, Guy knew that, and he knew that the profession was so steeped in tradition that the various jobs were handed from father to son, from generation to generation.

"What does San Benito want?" Guy asked.

"I don't know," Marcos shrugged. "He called, and he'll be here in about an hour. He asked that you meet him. It could be a big break for us. You'll hang around?"

"Sure," Guy stood up, winking at Marcos. "But, right now, I want to go see a woman about a cat."

Marcos grinned, "Watch out for those pussies, they bite. But, then who am I to be telling you? Be back at this table in one hour, right?"

"Right," Guy gave Marcos a comrade's shoulder slap, and started worming his way through the crowded room. All at once, he was alone and fair game for the roomful of fans. A girl shoved an autograph book toward him, "Su signatura, El Oro!"

He scribbled his name on a blank sheet, and there was a second and a third, before a heavy-set man pushed his body between Guy and the girls.

"Excelente, Senor," he threw his arm up, hooking his hand on Guy's shoulder. He seemed vaguely familiar to Guy, before he recognized him as the Mexico City scout. "You were very good today. I've been talking to your manager. We may be seeing you in El Plaza de Toros soon."

"Gracias, Senor," Guy said politely. "Now, I've got to run. Someone is waiting for me."

He winked, "A woman, I hope."

"Perhaps, Senor," Guy said. "Qui sas."

"Bueno!" he beamed, and stood back as Guy worked on through the crowd. They liked him; every person in the room, with few exceptions, liked Guy Moran. It was easy for him to forget about Texas and the dust and the wind, because right now, he was a hero. He did not try to analyze their actions, he just knew that they liked to touch him. He slowed his step, and shook hands with a tall man, standing beside a very well-dressed woman. She was an American, and the man was Mexican, and obviously wealthy. No one on earth knows quite so well how to be rich, as the playboy son of a wealthy Mexican family.

"Eduardo San Benito, Senor," the man pumped his hand. Turning to the woman, "Alice Kantrell, from your country. In fact, from your state."

"Texas?" Guy asked.

"Dallas," Alice Kantrell spoke to Guy, but she was looking at his body. She must have liked what she saw, because the smile on her lips was for real. "We'll be seeing you at the ganaderia soon, I hope."

"Good," Guy started to move away, "Perhaps we can talk about places and people."

"Id like that, very much," Alice said, smiling.

Eduardo San Benito waited until Guy was beyond earshot, then he turned on Alice. "You did not have to be so obvious. Now he knows that you'd like to roll around in bed with him."

Alice's face was a blank, "He should make a very interesting addition to one of your parties, Eduardo. Why, even your virgin sister might go for him."

"She might," Eduardo speculated, "but I doubt it. She's not his kind of woman."

She laughed, "Don't be an ass, Eduardo. Any woman is his kind of woman—and, they all like it. But, don't be jealous, darling, there's just one of him, and even gods get tired after awhile."

CHAPTER FIVE

"I DON'T BELONG HERE," the woman reporter picked up her bag and met Guy as he came into the private room. "I crashed this party."

"So?" Guy stopped her, holding her shoulders in his hands. "It's my party."

"You're not going to like me," she said.

"Why?" Guy glanced at her bag, "Because you're a reporter? I've met lots of reporters, good and bad, but I've rarely seen one as pretty as you."

"I came here to do a personal article on you," she said. "A confidential article about what kind of man you are. You're somewhat of a surprise, if you want the truth."

"How's that?" Guy asked.

"I don't know what I really expected, American bullfighter and all, but you're different from what I thought." She dropped her bag in an empty chair, turning away from Guy.

"I thought you were Mexican," Guy said.

"I'm Mexican-American," she said without turning. "I'm from Los Angeles."

"Do you still want to find out what kind of man I am?" Guy took a step toward her, and when she did not turn to face him, he moved closer. He came up behind her, grasping her shoulders and turning her.

Her feet twisted, and she fell against him, but was quick to step back, "Listen mister, I don't know if I do want to write an article about you. I saw how you treated those people out there, as if they were from another planet or something, and you were just there. I bet you couldn't tell me a thing that was said at the table where you were sitting."

"You'd lose your bet," Guy said flatly. "I know what was said at the table, very well. I might not like some of it, but I know. I'm not stupid."

"Who was that goog-eyed girl, who practically had sex with you at the table?" She asked watching for his reaction.

"Bambi?"

"I don't know her name, rank or serial number," she snapped. "The other woman was your wife, I know that much."

"What does it all mean to you?" Guy asked.

"It means that you're all involved in a crazy-mixed up affair, and if I have good sense," she walked across the room and looked out the window, "well, if I do what my mind says, I'll get the hell out of here."

"What tells you to stay?" Guy started toward her; she whirled and held up her hand to stop him, like a traffic cop.

"My curiosity says stay, and find out if the rumors are true."

"Rumors? About me?" Guy grinned, "They probably are."

"You're a real lady's man, aren't you?"

"It didn't start out that way," Guy said quietly, and it sounded more as if he were thinking aloud, than giving her an explanation. He stopped short, before he told her anything confidential. What the devil was wrong with him? he asked himself. Here he was talking to a complete stranger as if she were a lifetime friend. "Look, maybe it was a mistake for me to come here after you. Perhaps we'd better call it quits, while we're still ahead."

"Why did you come in here?" she asked flatly.

"Do I have to tell you?" he retorted. "Why were you waiting?"

She laughed, "Probably for the same reason. You intrigue me. I thought it might be nice to find out for myself just what kind of man you were. I didn't like the exhibition I saw out there. It was boring, I thought you'd at least be different, but I should have known that you were just another clod, who's brought a little attention to himself. And I came all the way from L.A., just on the chance there might be some excitement with you."

Guy looked at her, and he was strangely excited by her talk. She was different, very different, and Guy was challenged by the way she handled herself. Up to now, he'd thought of just one thing: sex, but now he was wondering just what this woman had in mind. Just how different did she want him to be?

She sauntered across the room and picked up her bag, "Well, listen, I'll see you around sometime."

Guy was quick on his feet; he grabbed her arm, twisting her back toward him. "What have you got on your mind?"

"Are you really interested?" she asked skeptically. "I don't think you'd like sex with me. I don't just fall back on the mattress and let a man bang away—I want something really exciting."

"Maybe I want excitement too," Guy said. "We might just make a real night of it."

She studied him carefully, and saw that he meant it. Guy saw the speculation in her eyes, and nodded. "I'm game for anything you can think up."

"That leaves me a pretty wide field," she commented.

"It takes two to play any game," Guy said. "What do you like?"

"I've got some pictures of what I like; want to see them?" When Guy indicated that he did, indeed want to see her pictures, she opened her bag and brought out three glossy prints. They were pictures of a man and woman together, and from the look on their faces, it was pure, sheer ecstasy which they were sharing, but the way they were having sex had, until now, been something which Guy knew about and considered disgusting. Still, with her, it might be different. He might be able to do, but he doubted it.

"This is way out," he commented.

"I thought it might frighten you," she said taking back the photographs. "Some men just can't do it, and I figured you to have a weak stomach. Well, you go back to your boredom, and I'll go back to L.A. where men are willing to experiment."

In spite of the way Guy felt about her way of having sex, he was excited. There had been something about her, which intrigued him from the first moment he saw her. She was beautiful and different, all over different, and now Guy was like a high school kid who's just had his first taste of liquor. It burned like all get-out, but he wanted more, because it was against the rules to drink under age. What she wanted to do was against the whole set of social rules, but it was different ... and exciting.

Sex was always exciting.

"You leaving now?" Guy asked.

She shook her head, "Nope. I leave tomorrow."

"What's your room number?"

She did not say anything as she looked up at him, then a thin smile spread her lips. She lifted one eyebrow, and Guy saw a flush in her cheeks. She might be very good. He didn't know yet if he'd go to her room, but she gave him the number and it was a room only four doors from his suite. When she was gone, Guy had the delicious experience of encountering something new and challenging. He did not know if he wanted to do it, or not—in fact, he automatically felt that he would go to bed and forget about her.

Guy was no fool about sex, and he knew that there was an almost infinite variety of sex habits, but he preferred the old standby: boy with a girl, and boy on the girl. But this was a strange profession, and there were all types in the clan of *aficionados* who followed bullfighters from town to town. There were the girls, always the same girls, perhaps not the same people, but the same kind of girls. All a bullfighter had to do was crook his finger, and they were naked at the count of one-two-three. He'd had his share of those, and they were like sawdust.

Then, there were the girls like Bambi and Marge, because Marge fell into that category in spite of their marriage. They knew the sexual ropes, and everything about how to make a bullfighter into a man, because there was a real difference between bull-fighter and man. They could almost be classified as artists; each knew the perfections and refinements of her sex, and employed them usually with just one man, on a give and take basis. Many bullfighters never went beyond this kind of arrangement, though the opportunities were wide and varied.

After these two types, it broke down into "special interest" groups. There were deviates, the *maricones*. Guy did not know of any bullfighters who were homosexual, though he would not have doubted that some of them liked to play around a little now and then. There must be some reason for the boys who were always there; even now, there were some in the outer room, at *his* party, and he wanted nothing to do with them.

Yet, he could understand the *maricones'* role in this life. When a man faces something as deadly as a charging bull week after week, months and years, it gets to the point where nothing excites him. Nothing is stimulating, and most of his excitement is self-induced or even forced. Men who live by excitement need excitement to keep on living, and Guy knew that even Bambi at her best was sometimes boring. It was not Bambi's fault, and she was as good as most and probably better, but he knew what was going to happen with her. He knew sex with Bambi, just as he knew the palm of his hand, and he could almost go through the ritual by rote. It was the same always, the initial jokes, the teasing touches, the tongue to tongue kiss, the warm caress, and the final physical act which began from the very beginning, and slowly gained momentum, until it left him exhausted for a moment.

Guy needed something which would leave him as exhausted in bed as he was after a three-bull fight. Perhaps once it could have been Bambi, but Guy was honest enough with himself to know that boredom was creeping into their relationship, and he knew that Bambi recognized this too.

And, there was the promise of tonight.

"Jesuchrist!" He said aloud, bashing his fist into the opposite palm, as he remembered Marge saying that she was coming to his room tonight.

She just might not find him there.

Guy almost winced at the explosion which would result, and then he laughed out loud as he pictured Marge's face completely frustrated. Marge stood up! It was incongruous, idiotic and perfect.

Good old Marge, stood up by her own husband.

"Guy!" He whirled as the door opened and Marcos poked his head in the room. He looked around, "Did you catch the cat?"

"Maybe," Guy conceded. "You got Don Juan San Benito out there?"

"Right," Marcos said, "And man, is he ever anxious to talk to you. You'd think it was you who was *dueno* of one of the big three ganaderias."

Guy laughed, "Maybe I just look important."

"You *are* important," Marcos said. "Just you wait and see the papers tomorrow. Man, they've made a hero out of you since this afternoon. We're on our way to the top."

"At least, we can see it," Guy said.

"Come on, Don San Benito is waiting," Marcos beckoned, and Guy went back into the crowded outer room. It was a crowd of friends, and thinning just a little now, so they cleared a way for Guy and Marcos without much shoving. Several stopped Guy for a word, but Marcos urged him on to the table where an old man with pure white hair, dressed in a perfect, black suit waited. Beside him, a tall, lanky Mexican sat with brooding black eyes.

They stood as Guy and Marcos came to the table, and Marcos beamed. "Don San Benito, El Oro, Guy Moran."

"Con mucho gusto, Senor," the old man reached and shook hands with Guy. "This is my nephew and general foreman and manager, Quiqui."

The name sounded like key-key, and Guy half expected the skinny man to rattle as he too shook hands. He turned back to Don San Benito, "I've met another man, who I presumed would be your manager."

"Who, Senor?" Quiqui asked quickly.

"Eduardo San Benito," Guy said. "No offense meant."

Don San Benito laughed pleasantly, "Eduardo is my son, he does nothing but play." He rested his hand on the taller Quiqui's shoulder, "I depend on Quiqui for everything."

"Eduardo does not stay at the ranch?"

"He stays," San Bento said, "But I discipline my bulls, not my children."

Guy looked at Quiqui, and knew that this was an important man, perhaps even the real power of the San Benito, Ganaderia. But, he liked Quiqui, regardless of his position with San Benito. The man was a cattleman who knew bulls as well as any bullfighter, and knew how to make good bulls. His skin was windtanned, and the lines around his eyes were from watching cattle in the bright sunlight. He extended his hand a second time to Quiqui, "It's a pleasure to meet a real man. There are too few."

A broad smile washed over Quiqui's features, and completely changed his attitude toward Guy. Until now, he had viewed the American bullfighter as a novelty, a here today, gone tomorrow flash on the scene. Somehow, they made contact, and Quiqui, like Guy, knew that this was a man he could respect.

"Sienten se, Senores," Marcos swept the chairs with his hand, "We need drinks." He clapped his hand and a new bottle of tequila and a fresh bowl of lemons appeared almost instantly. The toasts were quick; they toasted the bulls, the bullfighters, the bull breeders, and the boys who became men when they faced the bulls.

It was after the fourth round of drinks that Marcos and Don San Benito had firmly established their rapport, and Quiqui and Guy were left more or less to a private conversation, while the old men discussed the better days of bullfighting.

Quiqui had begun to relax, when Guy suggested they find something to eat in order to blunt the impact of all the tequila. He agreed, and they left the old men and went into an equally ornate dining room on the opposite side of the hotel lobby.

"We're having a tentadero," Quiqui said over cold shrimp and black coffee. "That's why we came, Don San Benito wants you to be there."

"It might be nice," Guy mulled. "The ranch would be quiet after these hotels."

Quiqui threw back his head and laughed, "You don't know the San Benito Ranch. There is nothing quiet about our ganaderia, not with Eduardo and his women and men. They come for a party and stay weeks. And, there is Vita."

"Vita?" Guy frowned.

"El Don's daughter," Quiqui seemed to savor the very mention of her name and position. "She is beautiful. beautiful. There is no other woman like her in all of Mexico. I would marry her, if I were not her cousin."

"That stops you?" Guy asked.

"Not me, Senor, but her," Quiqui confided. "Don San Benito has only two children, her and Eduardo. He has a big, big family, enough to fill this room," Quiqui flayed his arms to encompass the entire dining room, "but only two children. Eduardo is useless, he would throw away everything if El Don left the ganaderia to him. He hopes that Vita will marry a man, who can run the ganaderia."

"Sounds like there would be plenty of applicants," Guy commented. "To take Don San Benito's place would take a lot of man."

"It would take the right man, Senor," Quiqui said seriously. "The right man would have lots of help, but the wrong man would have lots of opposition."

"How do you stand?" Guy asked.

"With my cousin, Vita," Quiqui said.

Their discussion was interrupted by Don San Benita and Marcos' arriving at the dining room. Even with too much tequila,

Don San Benito was the personification of old world dignity. He drank like a gentleman, he walked like a gentleman, and every movement and word showed that he was a gentleman.

"Did Quiqui tell you of the tentadero?" He asked Guy, and repeated Quiqui's invitation to take part in the event. The tentadero was an essential part of a ganaderia's operation. Like everything else connected with the business, Guy knew that the tentadero was steeped in tradition. The breeders of fighting bulls tested their calves for bravery at the tentadero, where a picador provokes a charge from each calf, male and female. Their bravery was judged by this test, and only the bravest were kept for stock for the ganaderia. The others were sent with common cattle to the slaughterhouse to be butchered.

Guy had often heard how they judged the caliber of a bull. The breeders believed that the fighting bull took his size and strength from his father, but the fighting spirit came from the mother. So, in a way, the tentadero could have an effect on bull-fighting for years to come. Special calf fighters called becerristas, were brought in to take the young females through cape work, so that a better judgment could be formed about her calves. Only the females went through capework at the tentadero; the young bulls were never allowed to charge a cape until the day they roared into a bull ring, and faced a man such as Guy. A bull who had been taken through capework, would be a killer in the ring.

Too, Guy knew that a tentadero was the cause for wild celebration, and he was intrigued by the San Benito family. This would be his first major tentadero, and it was a pretty sure sign that he was headed for the top of his profession.

"You will come, Senor?" Don San Benito asked.

"Como no, Don San Benito," Guy accepted the invitation. "I am honored."

"Not you, Senor," Don San Benito said, "It is we, who are honored by so popular a torero. I've made all the plans with Marcos."

"Bien," Guy shook hands with him.

"Hasta la vista," Quiqui saluted him. "It will be worth your coming."

"Until the tentadera," Guy said.

Marcos stood with Guy until they left, hardly able to contain his excitement. To Marcos, this was the most positive sign of Guy's acceptance into an otherwise all-Mexican group. There were other American bullfighters, but not those who were invited to a tentadero at the ganaderia of Don Juan San Benito. He practically leaped on Guy when they were gone, "We're there, Guy. We've made it! Only Mexico City is left!"

In a way, Marcos was right.

Yet, Guy felt strangely emotionless about the whole thing, as if he knew from the very beginning that sooner, or later, they would be coming to him. Now that they were, it did not mean near what he thought it would, in the beginning. He left Marcos and walked upstairs toward his rooms, trying to sort out his feelings now. He should have been triumphant; there was nothing he could not have. There was plenty of money, lots of women, and he could take his choice of them for sex. It seemed impossible that there was a time in his life when he would have been grateful to any woman for sex, but there was, just as there is in every man's life. Things had changed radically for the Guy Moran who grew up with sage and sand.

It was almost as if he were two different people.

And, upstairs, the wife of both of them was waiting, early and impatient. Marge had guessed that Guy might try to give her the slip, and old Marge might be nodding now and then, but she was far from asleep.

"Hello, lover." She met him in the hall, "Anyone in your bed?"

"Not that I know," Guy said, disappointed that she was there.

"Good," she smiled. "Then let's you and me go talk about things like money and marriage."

CHAPTER SIX

MARGE STARTED STRIPPING as soon as Guy closed the door. She kicked her shoes off, and they clattered across the floor. Guy watched as she draped her blouse over the back of a chair, and began to struggle with the button and zipper of her skirt.

"Aren't you in a hurry?" He asked.

She chuckled, "Might as well get down to business."

"What's the matter," he asked, "Isn't Tacon giving you any these days."

"Enough," she grinned, "But you know, even though I love caviar, sometimes I get a real hankering hunger for bread and meat. You're like that, lover, you're just a plain, simple, red-blooded American, but you're a good lay. Once in awhile, I like it your way."

"Maybe I'm not so hot to trot," Guy suggested.

She came toward him, "Remember me, lover? I'm your wife — now kiss me." He did, for old time's sake, but there was just no spark in it for Guy. Marge was still an attractive woman, he would admit that and Tacon would confirm it—Tacon and a whole series of others.

She sensed his reluctance, and broke their kiss before it had a chance to pick up speed. It was not going very far anyway. "My, you can be a cold fish, lover." She studied his face. "Let's have a drink. You got anything?"

Guy nodded, "There's some Scotch in the bureau. I'll fix it."

"No, no," Marge shook her head. "I'll fix it. Let me do my monthly wife-duty."

"You can skip it," Guy suggested.

"Are you kidding?" Marge walked across the room and jerked open the bureau. There was a bottle, half-full, and Marge broke the cellophane wrappers on two hotel glasses. The sound of the paper ripping was the only sound in the room, as Guy sank into a chair and watched his wife. She was dressed in her half-slip and bra, her hair was loose on her shoulders, and Guy had to admire her hip movements. They had always been good, and Marge was a perfectionist.

"Lover, call downstairs for some ice," she said over her shoulder. "I hate hot whiskey."

Guy reached for the phone, as Marge picked up her bag. Snapping it open, she searched inside until she closed her fingers over a bandaid-size package of whitish powder. While he was giving the order, Marge opened the packet and sprinkled an almost microscopic amount of Spanish Fly in Guy's Scotch.

"It'll be up in a sec," Guy replaced the phone. "Want to talk?"

"Um-hm," Marge nodded, sitting on the edge of the wide bed. "Lover, did you ever give any thought to us as a twosome again? I mean, we could live together, you know."

It sounded suspiciously like Communist co-existence to Guy. He might be the "co"part, but Marge would do all the existing. "Wouldn't that put a cramp in your 'relationship' with Tacon? It would look sort of funny, you know, with us together and Tacon always there for breakfast."

"I don't mean it that way," Marge stood up and came toward Guy. She walked slowly, until she was behind him, then she put her hands on the slope of his shoulders, at the base of his neck, and began to massage him. Her hands worked, kneading his muscles, and it felt good to Guy.

"What do you mean, then?" Guy asked.

"Oh, lots of people live together, with an understanding." Marge's hands worked rhythmically. "Just because we don't believe in 'me for you, and you for me, and no one else,' doesn't mean that it's the end of the world. I heard two of those reporters talking about a divorce. I don't think I want a divorce."

"Is that why you're here now?" Guy mumbled, enjoying the massage.

"Partly, but like I said, sometimes I like to come home and see if everything is still in order."

"The plumbing works fine," Guy laughed, just as a knock shattered the mood Marge was creating in him. She opened the door wide to the bellboy, who recognized her. There was a look of surprise on his face, as he put the ice on the bureau and Marge tipped him. It was all calculated, because Marge knew that bellboys talk, and she wanted this one to talk; it would have a good laxative effect on a lot of divorce talk which threatened Marge's financial status.

She plunked two cubes in each glass, and mixed Guy's with the tip of her finger. "Ummh, good Scotch, lover."

"We can afford it," Guy said, taking his glass and sipping the mellow whiskey.

Marge sat opposite Guy, sipping her drink, waiting for the effect.

She did not have to wait long.

Guy had no intention of having sex with Marge, when he first encountered her in the hall, but now something was happening to him. He was beginning to feel a prickly heat, and a burning sensation in his groin. Marge came toward him and just her touch excited him.

She sat down in his lap, lifting her lips to him for a kiss. Guy took her, pulling her hard against him, and hungering for the feel of her flesh against him. This was his woman, he was married to her even if she was a tramp, and right now, he wanted his part of the bargain. It was a quick switch for Guy, but the way he felt, he did not give a damn that he had been tricked.

He was going to have her. All the forces of Hell would not stop him now. He jammed his lips harder over her mouth, and

Marge squirmed in his lap. His tongue groped beyond the ridge of her teeth and took demanding possession of her mouth. Marge almost felt that she had unhitched a hurricane, and pushing with both arms, she broke his kiss.

"For God's sake!" she exclaimed, "You don't have to rape me!"

"Come here," Guy ordered.

She backed away from him, moving toward the opposite wall. Guy stood up and started toward her, "You doped my drink," he accused.

Marge felt uneasy and just a little apprehensive about what she had one. "I put just a little—"

"You put Spanish Fly in my drink, didn't you?" Guy moved toward her, and Marge inched back to the wall.

"Just a little, Guy," she said, "I just wanted to make you feel a little more friendly. Maybe I got too much. Guy, for God's sake control yourself!"

He was in control of himself.

At first Guy did not realize what had happened, but Guy had been in Mexico too long not to recognize the effects of the aphrodisiac, and Marge had not known what Guy's reaction would be. It angered him,—naturally he reacted with sexual stimulation, he would have had to be made of concrete to resist that, but more than anything, it angered him. Guy hated trickery, and Marge had pulled some—being too unsure of herself to rely on her own body.

He'd give it to her, and give it to her good, until she begged him to leave her alone.

"Guy, please," Marge looked panicky as he grabbed her wrist and heaved her toward the bed. "Just take it easy, Guy, you don't know what that stuff will do!"

"I know what it'll do," Guy said, "And I know what you've done. It was a lousy goddamn thing to do."

"Just take it easy, Guy," she smiled nervously. "I've never held out on you, and I won't now. After all, I'm your wife."

Guy wanted to hit her, to slap hell out of her, but his excitement was greater than his anger. It was a sick thing, and Guy knew it, but he was going to satisfy the grinding heat of his body, and at the same time he was going to make Marge crawl. She knew it, and she felt as if she were going to be pulverized, but Guy was important. He was a helluva lot more important than Tacon or any of the others who came before Tacon. Guy paid the bills.

"Touch me, Guy," she smiled testily, "Make me like it, Guy, you know how. Play with me."

She was stretched on the bed, her hands lifted to him, and Guy gave in to an irresistible urge to fondle her. Touching her was no new experience, but with the pounding heat in his blood, Marge felt delicious and wonderful. Her skin was smooth and white, and Guy leaned over her, kissing her hard and aggressively.

She groaned and coiled her arms around his neck, wriggling beneath him, butting her hips against his legs. Now it was more than the aphrodisiac, it was male lust for female, and female hunger for him. His hands moved over her body, probing until he broke the fastener on her bra and her breasts peaked high and naked. He lowered his hands to her hips and stripped away her slip and panties. Her thin hose slithered off her legs, and Guy tossed them into a heap on the carpet.

"You still like me, Guy?" she asked, her voice a lusty groan now. "Touch me, all over, Guy. Like you used to do; make me want to claw the walls."

"I'm not playing games," Guy said firmly, "You wanted it this way, I'll give it to you, just like you wanted it."

"Guy, please—"

"Shut up!" He clamped his hand over her mouth, and his other hand began to explore places which he discovered long ago, but each time he went over her body, it was exciting. He moved his hand up her leg, higher and higher, then dropping his hand from her mouth, he cupped her breast and began to squeeze harder and harder.

She whimpered with pain in her breasts, but Guy knew Marge. This was the way she wanted it; the pleasure of one hand offset the pain of the other. He dug his fingers like piercing steel into her flesh, and she seemed to become a creature of pure passion.

She threw herself against him, shoving him back on the mattress. Hovering over him, her breasts resting on the naked expanse of his chest, she began to kiss his body. Her lips touched his throat, drove down to the valley of his shoulder and swept the curves of his chest. She pressed her warm mouth to the flat of his abdomen. Nuzzling her cheek on his hard muscles, she looked up at him.

"God, Guy, there never was a man like you," she gasped. "Nobody could ever make me feel like this. I want to do everything with you, just everything. I feel so good, all over I feel good. Nobody knows how to do it like you, Guy. I love it. I want to do it until I go crazy. It just drives me nutty when we're like this—"

"Quit talking," Guy touched her lips, "Let's do it."

She touched him, squeezing him, and Guy's body went rigid as she fondled him. Abruptly, Guy knew that she was going to do something which they had never done before, and he felt like stopping her, because it was going to sicken him, but he knew that it would be wonderful.

Slowly, she began to do it.

It was something Guy had never done, never thought he would do, but it was incredibly sensational, unbelievable. It was perfect for the flood of excitement which possessed him, and he did not want her to stop.

He did not know where she had learned it, but it was terrific and amazing, and he felt one wave of sensation crashing on another, as she went on and on, and on.

He touched her hair, as her hands moved over his body and she explored all of him. Her fingers combed through the longer hairs of his legs, and moved up to cup him.

It was better with every movement, unexplainably he knew that it was right for Marge. This was her, and he threw himself back, yielding his body to every move and touch of her lips.

His entire body seemed to prickle with excitement.

It was better.

Better.

She moved faster and faster, and suddenly Guy's head reeled as explosive sensations flooded through him. There had never been anything like it before, never, never, never. It was breathlessly wonderful, too great to explain, and he could only lie back as sheer exhaustion swept over him. Marge lay inert for a moment, resting her head on his stomach, her hair brushing his chest with each gasped breath.

She raised her eyes, "Like it?"

"Couldn't you tell?"

She pushed herself to a sitting position, fanning her hair with her hand. "I guess all of us have a little of it in us, even you."

"What do you mean?" Guy raised on one elbow.

"Oh lover, don't be a prig!" She exclaimed. "You don't think it was the first time for me, do you?"

"You knew what you were doing," Guy said. "What other tricks do you have up your sleeve?"

She laughed, "Lover, for people like us, people who thrive on excitement, there have to be different ways. If we just went along with the same humdrum stuff, we'd go batty." She patted his stomach, "Now wouldn't you? Don't you like a little experiment, now and then?"

"What kind of experiment?" Guy asked.

"This was nothing," Marge grinned, "Compared to some of the stuff I've seen—and, done," she added as an after thought. "Down here, they know how to make it real exciting. I never dreamed it could be so wonderful. You should get in on some of these parties."

"Thanks, but no thanks," Guy sat up. "I might not have the stomach for it."

Marge laughed loudly, "That just goes to prove what they say."

"What do they say?" Guy demanded.

Marge turned to him, grinning, "Do you know what the people in the business call you? *Bl Padrel* You're a damn puritan!"

"Me," Guy touched his chest, *"A puritan?"*

She laughed again, "Your morals are almost as modern as the Model T. You think you're really bad, just because you have a Bambi around in the closet." She reached to his face, patting his cheek. "Guy, honey, you're just a babe; that's why it's fun to be with you. You're so surprised and excited when we do something like this, when it's old hat to a man who knows his way around the sheets."

"Like Tacon?" Guy asked, hardly keeping the sarcasm out of his voice.

"Lover," Marge stood up and started dressing, "If you were half as good in the ring, as Tacon is in bed, you'd already be *Numero Uno!*"

"You bitch!" Guy snapped.

He felt disgusted with her; all the excitement of what they had done was gone, and now he felt sick at his stomach. If there was nothing, just what did she know? What did they do to amuse themselves? How much further could they go? And, he wondered why he was sinking with them? What was he looking for, anyway?

Certainly not Marge or Bambi.

"Padre, got any more Scotch?" Marge picked up her glass and held it out to him. "Why we might even work up a second wind for you. Rumor has it that you die after one time at bat. It must be dull."

"Get out of here!" Guy grabbed her and started shoving her toward the door.

"Now wait a goddamn minute!" Marge hissed.

"Get out," Guy shoved her toward the door again, "Or I'll beat you to a pulp."

She took a stance at the door, "Aren't you the big, tough he-man! Can't take it, can you, El Padre?" She laughed at him now, and Guy was shaking with fury.

"I mean it, get out."

"Not until I'm ready," she said. "I'm your wife, remember?"

"How could I forget?" Guy asked, "But, get out."

"No."

"You're asking for it."

"Give it to me!"

And, to her surprise, Guy did. He shoved her out the door, tossed the rest of her clothes through the transom into the hall, and, while she pounded on the door, he went to the john and was sick at his stomach. Maybe, just maybe he'd get used to it. He wished he had never learned about it, because he knew he would be propelled toward it, just as surely as he permitted what happened with Marge.

He was like a man standing on top of a tall building, staring down, knowing that if he fell he would die, but unable to stop his gaze.

Guy did not know what was going to happen to him; he could never have guessed that only four doors down the hall, another woman was talking about him.

"You know," Susanna, the dark haired reporter looked at the languid form of the young novillero, Tacon, "I met your Marge's husband. He looks exciting."

Tacon laughed, "Marge says he's as dull as stale bread."

She shrugged, drawing on a yellow papered cigarette, "I can change that."

"I doubt it," Tacon said. "Marge is a hot number herself."

"I'm going to try," she said, and Tacon joined her in a smoky toast to her ability. He might doubt she could, but she knew better.

She would change Guy, and she was planning it, just as general plans a war, and she was ready for the first battle. "I wonder just how far he'll go?" She asked, but Tacon was already asleep, and the question was not really for him, it was her question to herself, and Susanna was going to find the answer.

CHAPTER SEVEN

I T WAS DARK OUTSIDE, by the time that Guy had regrouped his emotions, and got control of himself. He was frank enough to admit that he was intrigued and curious about what Marge had partially revealed to him. Perhaps it was the partial view—had he known everything, there would have been no excitement about it. He tossed the idea of himself as a puritan around for awhile, and found it mildly amusing. He thought he led a pretty active life, but apparently he was pretty tame.

It was really funny, his wife telling him that he was "old hat." It was so goddamn funny that Guy decided to get drunk, and started with the remainder of the Scotch. There was not much, and it did not go very far, and it certainly did nothing to improve his disposition. He was going to have to get a lot drunker, before he could get over his reaction to Marge.

Guy stalked to the window, overlooking the street; it was festival night down there. The bullfight by itself was cause enough for a celebration, and Guy frankly wished that he could get that much pleasure out of something as simple as a bullfight.

Jaded. That was the word for himself and their whole crowd, except possibly for the peons of his cuadrilla. They were family men, dragging their wives and kids along to every fight. They were the proud owners of dumpy, fat wives and dirty faced kids, who prayed all during the fights ... the women hardly ever saw a fight, they just prayed and prayed, and everyone in the cuadrilla except him had a woman in the chapel. Every bull ring had its small chapel to the Virgen de La Macerena, and there the sounds of the fight gauged the intensity of the Aves.

It meant absolutely nothing to him, Guy told himself. He was not like them, he was not like those people on the street below him either. They got their kicks from simple things. Well, he'd had the simple things, and his life was one hellava lot more complicated. Still, he felt almost nostalgic as he watched them dancing and laughing on the street.

What the hell, he chided himself. Here he was, standing like a lovesick teen-ager, mooning over something which was impossible for him. He had been through that simple stage, and now he was standing on the threshold of something new. It just might be fun to play Marge's game, and beat her, with her own cards.

He dropped the curtain back in place, belted the last of the Scotch, and grinned to himself.

Whatever it was that Marge was talking about, he was going to discover it. Maybe, it would be enough to put some sort of meaning to everything—he muttered a curse word. Why was he always looking for something "stable" in his life. Hell, he'd had stability with his old man, and with the goddamn Army and then with dear old Marge. Stability was not what it was stacked up to be, he told himself. He had all there was to have. He was successful, there was plenty of money, and he could take his pick of bed partners.

He remembered the woman from California. The reporter.

She mentioned doing it differently, too. Really differently. Guy did not think he was up to it, tonight anyway. He slipped on his coat, and took the elevator downstairs. He wanted to find a liquor store open, and maybe he'd find something which would interest him.

The way he felt, she would have had to be the Queen of Sheba; he was dog-tired as he left the hotel and began shouldering his way toward the main plaza.

Guy took one glance at the town, and then tried to ignore it. It was a town, just like all the other small towns in Mexico. Twenty-five years ago, someone made an effort to pave the street which ran in front of his hotel, past the plaza and on to the bull ring. That meant that it was the main street, because the others were, more than likely, powdery dust.

Rows of naked lights were strung across the street, and seemed to be leading somewhere. Guy followed them, as far as the first bar, then he turned under the vivid red sign: "Bebidas."

The bar was long and narrow, and crowded with an about half and half male-female crowd. The only thing missing from the "picturesque" scene were the sombreros, and that might have interfered with the grey cloud over their heads, which grew larger and darker with each puff of every cigarette. Guy's eyes fought to adjust to the dark and the smoke, and he started for the bar, when he felt a hand on his arm.

"Where are you going, Torero?"

He whirled to see the girl from L.A. He blinked, "Well, hello, I didn't know you inhabited bars. I thought that would be too common for a sophisticated Californian."

"You can be nasty," she said, "can't you?"

"When I try," Guy nodded toward the long bar, Drink?"

"Naturally," she moved beside him, and Guy was very aware of her body, in spite of his own tiredness. She lifted one leg, and rested her well-shaped rear on a torn bar stool, then put her elbow on the rail. She opened her bag, took out cigarettes and was groping for her lighter, when Guy struck a match and held it cupped for her. She sucked the flame to the cigarette tip, looking down at Guy's hand. Slowly, she looked up, releasing the smoke through her nostrils.

"You've got nice hands, Torero."

"What's your interest in me?" Guy asked bluntly.

"Don't you think we ought to exchange first names, before we get down to interests and etchings and that?" She smiled. "I don't think you know my name."

Guy chuckled; he did not. "Call me Guy."

"Susanna." She twisted on the stool, and Guy wedged himself on the next seat. A fat Mexican was pushing against him, so he inched toward Susanna. She reached to smooth a wrinkle on her thigh, and her hand brushed Guy's leg. He looked up.

"Like I asked, what's the big interest?"

She ordered straight whiskey, and Guy ordered Scotch, paying with a twenty peso note. He waited for an answer; finally she drew deep on the cigarette, exploded the smoke and began to answer him. "It's a long story; want to hear it?"

"I'm here," Guy said. "Talk."

"I told you I'm an article writer. That's not the complete truth. I work for a scandal rag, exposing big names. I've seen just about everything, and I've done all of it. I was bored, and when I saw you, I thought maybe there was something more in it for me than a story."

"Why should you want me?"

She turned to him, "Confidentially?"

"No," Guy shook his head, "Honestly."

She waved her forefinger, "There is a difference."

"I know, but you can guess that I'm not going to lay myself open to a woman who's going to spread the dirt like feathers in a windstorm," Guy said.

"I told you, I'm not interested in the story." She swirled her drink in the glass. "All I could write about you has been 'exposed' a thousand times. People like different things, spicy and challenging. You're no challenge to my readers."

"I guess that about settles it," Guy commented. "You going to cue me in on why I'm the fair-haired chosen one, when you could probably tag anyone you wanted."

"I can," she said, "and I want you."

"You haven't told me why," Guy repeated his probe.

"Okay, just listen," she finished her drink and set the empty glass on the bar. Guy beckoned for the bartender to give her a refill, and waited. "When a girl like me has been around the Horn several times, she gets bored—"

Good God! Guy thought it was like listening to Marge.

"—I was in with a bunch of creeps in L.A. I wanted something new and lively. It's going to sound real perverse to you, but sometimes it's fun to initiate someone into all the sex goodies that a girl knows. I think you're a challenge to me. I expected to find some jaded lover-boy, instead, I found you—"

This was the second time today, that a woman had inferred he had a lot to learn about sex. It was beginning to damage his masculine pride.

"Maybe I'm happy," Guy broke in.

"I doubt it," she said. "We're a different breed from most people. What you've been doing is for the 'Johnny Hayseeds.' " She threw her arms wide, "There's a great big world of excitement waiting, but it takes sophistication to do it. You can't expect to enjoy it, and come out with your old-fashioned virtues intact."

"Who's virtuous?" Guy laughed, "Not me."

"Maybe I'm an iconoclast," she grinned. "I like to wreck people's playhouses, and rip down the old pictures and give a guy some new ideas."

Guy nodded; he could use a little something new. The Scotch was making him feel a lot better, and with each drink he was feeling more and more like taking her up on her proposition. Maybe they could find a common meeting ground, but as he looked at her, Guy knew that it was all the way with this gal; there would be no half measures.

It was no good tonight. For the things she wanted, he would have to be drunk or desperate, and he was just plain tired. He belted his drink, "I'm going back to the hotel. Maybe we can get together sometime."

She glanced up and down the bar, "I'm going to stay on for a little while. Couple of interesting characters down there."

"See you sometime?"

"You're going to the tentadero, aren't you?" She asked, Guy nodded, "Well, I'll be there, too. Eduardo is a friend; he says it should be a real ball."

He looked at her quizzically, but she had already turned to scan the line of faces at the bar. She was a strange cookie, turning her interest on and off like a light switch. It was "off" for him right now, but she had made it plain that she was coming to the San Benito ganaderia. He mused over the prospects as he walked back to the hotel. Just across the plaza, he stopped and bought a fresh bottle of Scotch, and the owner recognized him.

"Senor Oro!" He exclaimed, holding the liquor toward Guy, then drawing it back. "Un momento, Senor!"

With that he scampered to a door, which hardly seemed big enough to accommodate his fat frame. It was covered with stained curtains, which the man held back with a chubby hand.

"Mama!" He shouted into the back, "Rosa!"

"Que?"

"Andale!" He shouted, motioning with his hand, "Hurry!"

Two women puffed into the liquor store, one a younger carbon of her mother, who was perfectly mated to the obese storekeeper. The man took his daughter's hand and drew her toward Guy, "Senor, mi hija, Rosa. Jou like my daughter, Senor? She is a good girl."

Guy nodded, "A beautiful girl."

It was a lie, but one of those political lies which work such miracles of diplomacy. The girl tittered, and covered her face with her hands. Her mother slapped them away. "Maybe you like to go with Rosa to the street dance?" The woman suggested, "She dances very good."

Guy nodded, "I'm tired, very tired from the fight today. I couldn't dance."

"It was a beautiful fight, Senor!" The man clapped hands over his chest. "Magnifico! You kill so good."

"Thanks," Guy apologized to Rosa, who was still giggling as her mother led her away. He took out money to pay for the bottle, and the owner refused his money. Guy insisted, knowing that the man needed the money a helluva lot more than he did, and when he got his change he noticed that the old fox had overcharged him two pesos.

The hotel seemed almost a sanctuary to Guy. The staff had dimmed the lights, and two militiamen stood at the main entrance. They too, knew Guy and saluted perfunctorily as he walked inside. There was no one in the massive, heavy lobby, except the night clerk, who was nodding at the desk. Then, he noticed the bellboy, the same one who had seen Marge in his room, and started to wake him and ask if she was still in the hotel.

Instead, he went up the stairs, two at a time, and sat for a moment in the mezzanine. The chairs were big and upholstered in plush which bristled and pricked Guy's skin, even through his trousers. He broke the seal on the Scotch, and, lifting it, he took a long drink then lit a cigarette.

The place was as empty as a tomb.

Downstairs, over the balcony, he could see everything happening in the lobby, and the most activity was a cockroach trail that led up the wall, which Guy knew was the divider between them and the kitchen. He preferred not to know if they were coming from, or going to the kitchen.

The second swig of Scotch tasted even better, and Guy felt like shouting out over the rail, and waking the old night clerk and bellboy. The bastards were dead, and he was dead...oh Jesuzz! He was getting drunk. He looked at the bottle, and was amazed to see that it was nearly half empty.

He must have been thirstier than he thought. He ought to go back to that fat s.o.b. who overcharged him and get another bottle, but the slob would want him to shack up with that giggling heap of blubber! Oh hell, no!

He found the staircase, and all the perfect grace of the bull-fighter was gone as he stumbled upstairs. He groped his way along the hall, until he found his door. It was locked! He groped for his key, but he'd left it some sonavabitchin' place and he couldn't find it. He turned back to go wake that night clerk. The old coot ought not to sleep on the job. Christ! If Guy went to sleep on the job he'd be one dead sonavabitch.

Just like the whole goddamn world, he'd be dead.

"Hello, Guy." He looked up at his name. It was that black-haired Susanna from L.A. She was following him. "Lost?"

Guy leaned against the wall, "No, just my key's lost."

"You're drunk," she said.

"Not drunk enough," Guy grinned.

"Come on," she slipped her arm around his waist and veered them toward her door. "You need to sober up, man. You're four sails in the wind."

"I'm not drunk enough," Guy insisted.

"For what?" She opened the door and pushed him into her room. Guy leaned against the wall, waiting for his head to clear a little, as she stepped up against him, and repeated her question. "Why do you need to be drunk?"

"To do what you like to do," he said plainly.

"Do you think you'd like it?" She asked.

"I don't know," he admitted.

"Some men don't," she sighed and stated to walk away from him, but Guy caught her and pulled her back.

"I've never met a woman like you before," Guy said. "You're a cold fish; you like a guy one minute and you cut it off the next. What are you, anyway?"

"Just let go of me," she began to break Guy's hold, but he jerked her against his chest, and clamped his lips over hers. She struggled, then relaxed, and their kiss caught on and Guy was spiraled into something he would never forget. She was exciting, like nothing or no one else he had ever known. He hated her and he was pulled toward her, all in the same breath, and now he was kissing her. She yielded to him, stroking him and pulling him deeper and deeper into the secret warmth of her lips.

"Have you ever done it that way before?" she asked.

Guy shook his head, "No."

"Now?"

To answer her, he began to move his hands over her body, and they came together by compulsion. She moved her hands along the lines of his body, and Guy kissed her lips, her ears and throat. He brushed his lips through the dark mass of her hair, and took deep breaths of the heavy perfume she was wearing. It intoxicated him as much as the liquor, and he began to undress her. She slipped her dress over her head, mussing her hair, but she shook it back in place as Guy stripped away her slip, and then she stood before him wearing nothing except her bra and thin panties.

"Undress," she told Guy, "I'll wait."

He slipped out of his shirt, and she turned, looking at him with frank admiration. His chest was broad, even for an American, and it tapered to a small waist. His skin was almost hairless, and the muscles of his chest and arms were strong and big. She walked toward him, "Let me help you."

Her fingers loosed the button and zipper of his trousers and she watched as he tossed them over the chair. He reached for her, taking away her bra with one jerk.

Guy gave in to the surge of excitement sweeping over him. He was about to start something he had never dreamed he would do, but he seemed to be beginning a new chapter in his life, and it was almost as exhilarating as becoming a man for the first time. This was sex sophistication, and he was anxious to complete his initiation. He took away her panties and dropped them with his shorts, and they were standing hip to hip, naked and warm, her hands stroking his back and his resting on the mound of her hips.

"Take off my shoes," she whispered.

Guy sank to his knees and removed her shoes, then he began placing his lips on each of her toes. Her feet were sweet smelling just like all the rest of her, and he edged his lips up the sweep of her arch, burying his kiss in the dip of her heel and then flicked his tongue up the line of her leg tendon, until he plunged his kiss into the valley of her knee.

He could feel the first shiver of her excitement, as if he were passing it from his body to her, through his lips. He kissed the crest of her knee, then moving his hands upward he gripped her hips, and sweeping his lips he moved up, up and up toward the very essence of her. She held him, hypnotized and they were creatures of shared passion.

He moved upward, flicking his tongue over the softer protected flesh of her thigh.

She stood breathless and regal.

Her hands gripped his shoulders, and seemed to pull him higher and higher.

He did not resist.

Higher, and on, up.

Higher.

A low groan pierced her lips as he became more and more insistent. She dug her nails into his shoulder, breaking the skin, but Guy was heedless of the pain as he riveted all of his attention on one thing. It was his claim, every part and particle of her would be his. He would be initiated now; he wanted it and he drove on and on.

She was the gate to everything which challenged him, and Guy knew that he was leaving behind everything that had previously excited him. He was Columbus and the New World, Balboa and the Pacific, he was the great conquistador riding in triumph to claim the Seven Cities of Gold.

Cibola—gold, the essence of everything was there, and he moved closer and closer, up and nearer.

Nearer.

She shivered like a leaf in a wild, twisting whirlwind, and he returned her exciting passion, letting himself be caught up with her. The blood in his head cleared the fuzziness of the liquor, and he yielded to the compulsive drive of his body over his mind.

Higher.

She felt warm to his lips.

She fluttered like a bird, holding him tighter against her, pushing against his progress toward her, as if she would prolong it for hours and hours. She would take it forever, and he drove past her barriers.

And then, he was there, and the ritual began.

It was sweet and exotic … and nothing anywhere, in all his life had been as exciting as this moment. Sensations flooded her body, and he could feel her thrills. It was right, she was driving against him, battering his last reluctance as he plunged deeper and deeper.

It was perfect.

It was the most revolutionary night in Guy's life, and she held him, as if she would die if he moved from her, and then he sensed a deeper rumbling, and he drove harder and faster.

The rumble began to sound like thunder, and suddenly lightening exploded in her and shot into his body like vivid erupting flashes from the very core of the earth. It came like red-orange lava, ripping open the sides of a coned volcano, sweeping down the incline of earth and devouring everything in its path.

They fell apart.

She collapsed in a trembling, sobbing heap on the carpet, and Guy touched her foot as he lay exhausted, gasping for his breath.

It seemed forever, but it was only minutes until she took his hand and led him to the bed. There, she yielded to him, opening herself wide and full, taking him with ecstasy and joy, and they clung together for hours and hours. He took her again, and then they slept. She woke, burrowing against the warmth of his body, and their passion sprang up again, and she yielded to him again. They worked against one another at dawn, and satisfied the flames between them, and then they slept.

It was late afternoon when Guy woke.

He showered completely, then briskly dried his body with a thick, soft towel. His legs felt sore but his mind was as clear as mountain air. He was a different man.

He had found excitement, complete and total stimulation. He had run the full length of his passions, and now his body was satiated.

When he dressed he returned to the bed. and she lay curled like an animal with the sheet covering her breasts. They were limp when she slept and Guy turned away before he shattered the pleasure he had known with her.

It had been great—he glanced at his watch. It was three p.m., and he knew that Marcos would be pacing the floor. They were to leave for San Benito today.

He stood over Susanna; it really had been an experience, but as he closed the door, he never expected to see her again. It was a one time experience, which he never intended to repeat.

CHAPTER EIGHT

GUY DID NOT REALIZE HOW COMPLETE was the slip he'd given Marcos until he found him, waiting in his room. Marcos had begun to worry about midmorning, and now it was late afternoon. With each hour that passed as Guy did not appear, Marcos' anxiety grew. Marcos was more than a good manager to Guy. He had begun work with him when there was practically nothing but promise; he had guided him through the first humiliating fights, when Marcos alone saw the American novillero's promise. It took someone like Marcos to get Guy where he was today. A weaker man, or a poorer manager, would have been satisfied with the provincial fights in bordertowns, existing on the novelty of his client. But, neither Guy nor Marcos would have been happy with that kind of arrangement. Guy wanted to be more than just a novelty, a bullfighting clown, and Marcos wanted him to be great.

They were a perfectly mated team for getting to the top, and it was no easy climb, especially for an American. There are a lot of open doors for Americans in Mexico, but bullfighting was one of the most clannish, closed groups Guy could have chosen. Very few others had gone ahead of him, and even fewer had been accepted by the Mexicans. Marcos had seen them all. He was young when bullfighting was at the peak of perfection in Mexico. He remembered the greatest of the great Toreros, Manolette. Marcos was just a gangling teen-ager when Manolete made his Mexican tours, but there had never been an experience which so thrilled him. He could close his eyes today, and still picture the thrill he felt on the day he saw Manolete. It was a hot day, and Manolete stood in the ring with his sad classic Spanish features, and then he began to fight. A few times in his life, a man sees perfect artistry. Marcos saw it then, and he never forgot it in all the years which came afterward. Sometimes he saw something which almost approached it in Guy's fighting, like the moments when Guy had the bull's will broken and his body bending to Guy's whim. When it was at this point, something of the artist took over in Guy, and he treated the bull with disdain, as if the fight were no longer even, and Guy would kill the groveling monster to put it out of its misery.

Marcos was no dreamer, he knew that Guy was not Manolete. Guy was good fighter, perhaps the most promising on the scene; he killed well, after an artistic fight, but there was something wrong. It was nothing in Guy alone, it was like a sickness in the profession; a Torero was no longer a man's man; he was a matinee idol, and Marcos had seen the effect on Guy.

In the beginning there had been endless hours of practice. Day in and day out, Guy had worked in the ring with his cuadrilla, perfecting passes which set the spectator's hair on edge. Now, he was on the way to the top. Guy was made.

Marcos knew approximately what had happened last night. When the managers got together for a strictly confidential bull session, they sometimes opened up their problems. Marcos was not the first to see his fighter change dramatically. Some said it was the terror of the fight itself, which left the fighter with no other excitement, no other pleasure which did not seem dull. There were two things a fighter could do. He could take on fight after fight, and shorten his life and career by several years, or he could try to find thrills outside the bull ring.

Marge could have helped, but Marcos considered Marge as hardly more than a prostitute. Marge was worthless in Guy's life, absolutely worthless. She was an expensive ball and chain, which did not serve the purpose of keeping Guy at home. It might have helped if Guy had children, but bullfighters do not make good fathers, they die too young, and Guy knew it.

But, Marcos reasoned that Guy needed to be more than just a popular Torero; that was why he did not explode at Guy when he came into the suite after having spent the night with Susanna. Still, he could not let it go by without some comment.

"Everyone has been waiting for you since noon," Marcos said. "Where have you been?"

Guy glanced at Marcos, "With a friend."

"It wasn't Bambi. She left for Agua Caliente this morning." Marcos mentioned Guy's next scheduled fight, except for a small one at Tacquil, which both of them wanted to cancel now. But that was impossible, as the contract was binding. Guy could not expect Bambi to go to a dump like Tacquil, it was worse than this—but, oddly, he no longer cared too much whether Bambi was there or not, and he was grateful that dear old Marge shuddered at the mere mention of Tacquil.

"You know," he commented, "I'm going to be alone at Tacquil."

Marcos shrugged; there was no need to pick at Guy, they were going to be late arriving at San Benito as it was. "You're not alone, the caudrilla will be there."

"Do you think their wives will follow them?"

Guy's question came as a jolting surprise to Marcos; he was unaware that Guy even knew that his peones were married. "I suppose they will—"

"Even to a dump like Tacquil?" Guy was thoughtful, and when he was thoughtful like now, it disturbed Marcos.

"Why?" He asked testily, "Are you in a bad mood."

"No," Guy grinned as if to reassure Marcos. "I was just wondering."

"They'll follow their husbands, even to Tacquil," Marcos said. "You know how it is with Mexican women—"

"How is it with Mexican women, Marcos?" Guy threw his personal things into a bag. His *trajes de luces, capotes* and the rest of his fighting regalia had long been packed by Paco and Jose. "Maybe I don't know Mexican women at all. I know Bambi, and a couple of others like her, but maybe I don't know women at all."

"Who *were* you with last night?" Marcos asked.

"A woman; you don't know her."

"Better than Bambi?" Marcos lifted an eyebrow, studying Guy.

"She made Bambi look like a beginner," Guy said, closing his case, setting it on end for the bellboy. "Well, let's go before it's dark."

La Ganaderia de San Benito was located forty miles north and twenty-seven east, and hardly ten of those miles were smooth pavement. Guy pretended that he was asleep, and though Marcos knew Guy well enough to know that he was not, it was easier to go along with the game. When Guy was like this, something had happened, and it was either very good, or very bad. Marcos could have probed and discovered which it was, but sometimes it was better not to know.

Guy himself did not know exactly how to classify what had happened. Thrilling. Different. Excitement. Erotic. He closed his eyes and the part of the evening he remembered flashed before him, with Susanna's face. It was not really Susanna; he did not connect what had occurred between them with a person. It was simply that the change which everyone had seen, was suddenly highlighted to Guy.

He saw himself; as if for a mental flash he had entered a third dimension and could take an objective look at Guy Moran, El Oro, the rising star of the bullfighting scene. He knew he was good in the ring, very good; in fact he felt confident that he could handle any comers who wanted a *mano a mano,* and that included Tacon.

He knew too that he craved excitement in his private life that equalled the tense, explosive nature of his profession. It was just normal; most guys got their kicks at home in private, after a dull day at a humdrum job. It was just the opposite for Guy; everything outside the ring had been an anticlimax until last night.

Still, he did not know if he was going to enjoy this world of sophisticated sex. It was a big question mark to Guy, but he knew one thing for certain. He was going to find out for himself. He knew that Susanna would probably be at San Benito; if not. Eduardo San Benito would be there and he was one of the sophisticates. The group very likely included the American woman he saw on Eduardo's arm, Alice Kantrell, the one from Dallas.

Guy smiled with closed eyes, relaxing in spite of the bumpy road, and when Marcos saw it he began to relax. This could be a very important thing, this tentadero at San Benito. Not every bullfighter was invited by Don San Benito to the ganaderia; it was a very distinctive honor, and Marcos had leaked it to the reporters, of course. Too, it was near Tacquil; he wished he had not contracted for that fight. It was a fill-in at best, even at the beginning of the season, but now, with Guy receiving so much publicity, a place like Tacquil was just a waste of time.

Or, so Marcos thought.

The main structure of the ganaderia was an enormous adobe house. It sat, sun-baked and bleached, on the crest of a small hill. Heavy, low shrubbery crowded the walls, almost obscuring the wrought-iron grille-work, and lining the curving drive which Guy's car took up the hill. They bumped over the cattleguard, and picked up speed as they started up. Guy woke, and rolled down his window. The scenery was dramatic and rugged, like most Mexican pasture, studded with bristling yucca plants, and crouching mesquites with lacy leaves moving in the gentle breeze.

The house was massive, but not clumsy, and Guy took it in quickly in the last light of day. It was sunset, and the fiery beams made the already red tile seem to be on fire, and gave a look of purple to the shadows. The leaded windows caught the sun's rays and bounced them back toward Guy, like sparkling eyes.

Guy could almost picture the interior. It was a home built by old and familiar wealth, and as Paco slowed the car, tall iron gates swung open, and he eased the car into the circle drive. It was the direct opposite of the pasture land; plush flowers bloomed helter-skelter, draping reds and yellows on the drive, and the walls of the interior were covered with vibrant floribunda roses.

The air was like heavy perfume, as a gray haired servant opened Guy's door and bowed low.

"Bienvenidos!" Don San Benito came to meet him, "Welcome to San Benito. We've been waiting for you."

"We were late starting," Guy said, looking around, "It is certainly beautiful."

"Yes, Senor," Don San Benito beamed, "it has been in my family for many generations. It was built when Mexico was a colony of Spain; it was the Viceroy's summer home."

"Very impressive," Guy said. "Behind this, stands a thousand fighting bulls."

"Ayiee!" Don San Benito exclaimed, "And tomorrow we will see them. Come now, I want you to meet my family; we have waited dinner for you."

Guy followed him up wide, tile steps, so polished that they caught his reflection. They passed through another iron gate, and were then in the house's interior. A long, wide corridor with a gleaming tile floor went through the house and ended in an enclosed patio. Along the corridor Guy saw massive tables with hand-carved legs, and in the light of a series of real candle chandeliers, he saw wide ornate gold frames with dark portraits of the other San Benitos. A suit of Spanish armor stood guard beside the door where Don San Benito waited. He saw Guy studying the hall, "Very beautiful isn't it, Senor?"

"Extremely," Guy said with genuine admiration.

Don San Benito shrugged, "Ah, but it is from another age, closer to me than to you. We don't live like that in Mexico anymore. This house is old, and the young ones don't like it. Eduardo prefers a modern apartment; he says the ganaderia is depressing."

"Eduardo will change," Guy smiled at the old man's concern. It was strange the Don could not remember back thirty-five years, when he probably wanted his freedom, too, from an old man who ruled here.

Only now, he was the old ruler.

"Qui sas, Senor," Don San Benito smiled. "My family is waiting."

The two massive doors opened with absolutely no noise, and Don San Benito stepped back to let Guy enter first. It was a huge room, and they entered on a higher level than the center of the room. It was a long rectangle, and the top level went around it on three sides. From where Guy stood, in both directions doors lined the upper level, and between each door, hung an oil portrait of the ganaderia's important bulls. The level was separated from the main part of the room by a low wall and series of exquisite moorish arches and fine stone lattice work.

Through the lattice, Guy saw the assembled San Benito family, and it was large.

Don San Benito touched his elbow, and they walked under an open arch into the main part of the room. "My family, Senor."

The first thing Guy noted was the vivid contrast between two age groups. The elders, like the house, were from another age, a little more graceful, but slower. The younger members were as American as hot dogs and Sears-Roebuck.

"My wife, Senor, La Dona San Benito," Guy watched the woman come toward him, with the perfectly smooth grace of an elegant animal. Her eyes were large and black, and in spite of her years, she was a beautiful woman. She smiled and placed her hand in Guy's, "Con mucho gusto, Senor."

Over her shoulder, Guy saw the family matriarch, and he had to keep his eyes from wandering to the May Queen of this December gathering. She stood behind the matriarch, and it was obvious that she was as acutely aware of him, as he was of her.

"My mother, Senor, La Dona Beatrice," Don San Benito went on as if he were unaware that Guy and the younger girl were immediately attracted to one another.

The old woman remained seated, and Guy approached her, "Dona Beatrice," he extended his hand. She placed a frail, lace covered hand in his, and with a gentle tug caused him to lean close to her.

Her body might have been a thousand years old, but the old woman's smile was bright and her eyes were wise. "You be careful with her, young man," she spoke softly in perfect English, "She's my granddaughter. And, don't pretend that you haven't noticed her. Vita is too beautiful for a man like you not to notice. You break her heart, Torero, and I'll break your skull."

It sounded like a threat, except for the sparkle in the old eyes. Guy shook his head, "I'm not a heartbreaker, Dona Beatrice."

"Posh!" She waved her hand, "I've seen your kind before. Thousands of them. Handsome toreros, and you're no good for a woman who wants a family. You live by bulls, and you will be killed by a bull."

"It's part of the business, Dona," he agreed.

Don San Benito broke in, "Come, Senor, my nieces and my daughter."

Guy went through the long series of introductions, half-heartedly shaking hands with a group of youngish girls, some who dressed too old, some too young, but none were interesting, until at last he was introduced to Vita.

He knew of her, from Quiqui's conversation the first day at the hotel. He had said that she was beautiful, but it was the understatement of the year, as far as Guy was concerned.

He had shaken hands with all the others with more or less enthusiasm, but now, he felt a tingle of excitement as Vita put her hand in his, with no show of shyness. It might not have been the "correct" thing for her to do, but she looked into his eyes, "I've been waiting for you."

"For how long?" Guy asked.

"Since Quiqui returned," she smiled, "Maybe even longer."

"Vita," Don San Benito nodded to his daughter, "Why don't you show Senor Moran to his room? He will want a few minutes before dinner is served."

"Come with me, Senor," she stepped closer.

"Just call me, Guy," he said. She touched her finger to her lips, and realized that every face in the room was turned on them. San Benito's unusual action was for Vita's sake, and to ease the atmosphere of the room.

Old Dona Beatrice tapped her cane as he and Vita left by a side door. Guy caught her parting words, directed to Don San Benito. "Juan, you are a fool!"

"Mama—"

Vita closed the door, pointed to a smaller hall, and walked beside him. His room was three doors down the corridor, and his suitcase was already on the bed. It was a Spanish bedroom, and Guy wondered if they ever built a small room. It was dominated by a hulking four-poster, with a silk and bold brocade canopy. On each side was a dark wood, carved chest, mounted with an ornate brass candlestick.

Vita crossed the room ahead of him, her footsteps muffled by the thick carpet, and opened the shuttered windows. The view was of a small garden, with a bubbling fountain, and dark green trees, which accented the lighter colored banana trees, waving their flat leaves in the air. A parrot's squawk was the only sound, other than the fountain, as Vita turned and sank into the window cushions. "May I stay a minute?"

"Isn't it unusual?" Guy asked, hesitating to open even his suitcase with her still in the room. It was not like him to be shy around any woman; perhaps it was the atmosphere of the ganaderia which was affecting him, but he felt like he was out of place with this woman in his bedroom.

She knew it and laughed, "I planned it this way. I wanted to be alone with you."

"What will Dona Beatrice say?" Guy grinned. "She warned me about you."

Vita laughed, and, by glory it was the nicest sound Guy had heard in days. It was genuine; there was not a thing faked or forced about her, and he liked her.

"You know, your grandmother might be right," Guy said. "You're a beautiful woman."

"And you're a handsome man," she said. "I like you."

Guy felt uncomfortable; he threw his suitcase up on the expansive bed, clicked open the locks, and worked furiously shoving his gear about the bottom of his case, with his back to her.

She watched him silently, waiting. Finally, she leaned toward him, "Do you not like me? Quiqui said you were a strange man, in a hurry. Is there something wrong with me?"

"No, of course not," Guy whirled. He snatched a shirt out of his case, just to have something in his hand. "It isn't that at all, it's just that, well it seems so strange to have you here—in this room."

"Are women strangers to your bedroom?" She asked.

Guy looked at her quickly. Was she—? Oh, hell no! He cursed his own thoughts; she could not be like Susanna, and Marge, and Bambi. She was nice, almost flawlessly beautiful as she sat there in the sunlight, the last gold rays catching in her hair like magic. Her eyes were large, and dark, and Guy had a feeling that she could see through him, as though he were transparent, like her white skin. Her lips were full, red and sensuous, and Guy wondered just how many, if any, men had tasted their wine and been intoxicated with the sweetness of her body.

He shook his head to clear his train of thought, "Look, I'm not your kind of man. I like you, but don't let it be anything else—"

She stood up and come toward him, "What else, Guy?"

Guy shrugged, "I mean, let's not get involved. I'm all wrong for you."

"How do you know what is wrong with me?" she asked, "maybe I know more about you than you'd think."

"Look," Guy turned and walked from her, "I'm no babe in the woods, you know. I saw your family out there—"

"El Oro," she used his popular name, "I know all about you." She was walking nearer, "I know bullfighting, like I know my own hand. I've read about you, seen your picture and everything, since the first time you stepped into a bull ring in Juarez to fight a calf. I've read the critics as they tore you to shreds, and I've seen them change until they couldn't say enough good about you. It was my idea for you to come here in the first place."

"You thought up this invitation?" Guy would have been angry, if it had been any other woman. He had thought it was on his skill in the ring.

Vita stopped, and put a chair between them, "Every girl has a man whom she loves and cannot love. In the United States it is the movie star and singers; for me it was bullfighters. One bullfighter, you."

"How old are you?" Guy asked.

"Eighteen," she lifted her chin defiantly, "A woman."

Guy walked to her, took her shoulders in his hands and turned her to face him, "I'm ten years older than you and I've got a wife. I don't belong with your people. I'm wrong for you."

"Kiss me," she whispered.

"I shouldn't," Guy answered softly.

"Why?" Her eyes were half closed, and her lips were ready, tilted to him, offering him the young fruit of her body.

"Because—" Guy hesitated, "Because a kiss might not be all I want."

"Then you do like me," she said.

"Very much," Guy said.

"Please, kiss me," she whispered, "now."

And, Guy did.

It was a gentle, tender kiss, almost shy, as though they were a boy and girl, kissing for the first time. Her lips were round and soft, mated to Guy's thin, hardlined lips, and yielding to him with the softest whisper of a passion which was still in control.

Before it got out of control, Guy broke their embrace, and stepped back. "Your family will be waiting for you."

She lifted her hand, resting her fingertips on his cheek, a wispy smile on her lips. "I'll go so you can change. I think I could love you."

Guy shook his head, "Please, don't—"

Before he could finish, she was gone, and he was alone. The vastness of the room seemed emptier, as though he might be lost in a huge, rich cave. He noticed it was dark, and the cooler night air was coming in the open window. He closed the shutters, and flicked on the electricity, wondering why they kept all the candles, unless it were just for decoration. It was, and he liked the room, as he began to adjust and get the feel of the house. Every house has its own personality, and Guy could sense this house's soul, perhaps even more quickly because he had lived so long in soulless hotels.

In spite of its size, the room was comfortable, and Guy made quick work of stripping and showering. There was plenty of hot water, and the towels were as vast as his bed. He liked the woman smell of the towels; it was one of the things which hotels could never provide, and it came only from a piece of linen laundered by a woman's hand.

It was a nice house.

It was a home.

He finished his bath, and stepped naked into the bedroom, and realized immediately that he was not alone.

Quiqui sat, his legs sprawled outstretched in front of him, his chin resting on his bony hands. "Saludos, amigo."

"Quiqui!" Guy exclaimed, "Good to see you; I'll be dressed in a minute."

"Take your time," Quiqui grinned, "Tonight everyone will wait for the celebrity."

"Are you being sarcastic?" Guy asked.

"Just truthful," Quiqui said. "How do you like Vita?"

"Was I brought here for her?" Guy asked, a hard note creeping into his voice. "I thought it was for the tentadero."

"It was a little of both," Quiqui confessed. "El Don told you that he disciplines his bulls, not his children, and it's true. Eduardo is a big disappointment to El Don, but Vita makes up for it. El Don's life centers around her."

"Then I am here for her sake," Guy said.

"No, not completely," Quiqui said. "You are a topflight bull-fighter, and the first American to be invited to the ganaderia. Vita's wishes influenced El Don's decision to bring you here, but only just a little. You are here, El Oro, because Don San Benito admires you, and the way you handle his bulls. If you were a sloppy fighter, not even Vita could have brought you here for the tentadero."

"Thank you, Quiqui," Guy said.

"No, Senor, not me," Quiqui stood up, "It is you, who is the artist. I'm just a breeder; a clumsy, skinny breeder of bulls, but I know an artist when I see him fight, and I saw your last fight."

He watched Guy finish dressing, then he slapped Guy's shoulder, "Come, amigo. The great San Benito family council is waiting to finish judging you, and there is a table, such as you have never seen, and it is loaded with food."

"So?" Guy said, "I'm not that hungry."

Quiqui laughed again, clapping his hand against Guy's shoulder again, "She'll be there, amigo. She'll be there, you can count on that."

CHAPTER NINE

"TONIGHT IS JUST A FAMILY DINNER, in your honor," Quiqui confided. "They like to do it up big for someone especial, and there is no one so important to our family as a bullfighter."

"Helps business," Guy teased. "Will there be many?"

It was Quiqui's turn to laugh, "Guy, you have never seen a family until you've seen a Mexican family. Everyone who will be at dinner is kin to me, and this isn't all of them. We really believe that blood is thicker than water."

They came into a small ante-room, where everyone was gathered and waiting for him. Don San Benito was standing in front of a fireplace, and Guy could not help but look up at the almost lifesize portrait of a huge, black bull. Don San Benito saw his gaze and followed it, "This is the greatest of our bulls, Senor. He was killed by Manolete."

"If I were a bull, and I were to die," Guy said quietly, "I could think of no more glorious way to die."

There was a look of genuine pride in Don San Benito's eyes as he came up beside Guy, "Spoken like a true matador, Senor. Now, let us dine."

As they started toward the dining room, Guy had just time to see Vita standing beside Quiqui. They were talking rapidly, and she was looking at him. When she saw his look, she smiled, and Guy might have flashed back some sort of signal except for Dona Beatrice, who came up beside him and slipped her arm through his.

"Do me the honor, Torero," she smiled. The family parted to let them through. She leaned toward him. "See all those young people here, they're idiots. In my day, we would not have made such fools of ourselves. Flashing smiles and signals across a crowded room! Posh! They might as well telegraph it to *La Prensa*."

"Perhaps — "

"No perhaps about it, Senor," she smiled. "Part of the art of love is the mystery, the intrigue. How can there be any excitement when it is so open and obvious? My goodness, we all know that Vita was in your room this afternoon. I presume you were gentleman enough to leave her virginity intact—considering that you are a married man."

"Dona Beatrice!" Guy turned to her in surprise, "I wouldn't think you'd —"

"Posh! Boy, don't you think I knew about those things, when I was Vita's age?" She grinned, "I may be old, but I'm not dead. Keep in mind, young man, that this is a very old, and very proud family." She sighed, "I suppose you know about Eduardo. That boy! He has a woman here from your country, and she's nothing but a streetwalker."

"I met Alice Kantrell," Guy said.

"So! You know her name," Dona Beatrice looked up at him. "I hope you're not her friend."

"No, Dona Beatrice, I only met her at the hotel," Guy had to fight back a smile, and did it successfully, because he knew that the old lady was very serious.

She shook her head, "Such people you just have to live with. I've always agreed with the old Don, God rest his soul, that ours was the best part of the whole bullfighting business. I suppose that you would disagree."

Guy escorted her to a chair at the right of the head of the table, held out the chair until she was seated, then took his seat next to her. To his surprise, Vita was seated across the long table, where they could look directly at one another during the long, sumptuous meal.

First came the wine and fish, then the main courses of beautifully done beef and pork, succulent Spanish Blue Quail and oysters. Heaping platters of sugary vegetables and rich, doughy Mexican bread were passed over Guy's right shoulder. He knew that it was all spread for his benefit, but then on second thought, when he glanced at Vita and saw the happy flush in her cheeks, he repaired his opinion, and gave the honors to her. He was part of the girl's wish, this was her evening. He leaned to Dona Beatrice.

"Is today *cumpli de anos* for Vita?" He asked.

She looked at him surprised, "How did you know it was her birthday?"

"How old is she?"

She chuckled, "Senor, she is eighteen, unmarried and almost an old maid. Your kind of man certainly is not helping at all."

Click. Click. Click.

A whole lot of things fell into a pattern for Guy with the information that today Vita was eighteen. It accounted for everything; the splendor of the meal, the imported wines, the family gathering, and even him as the guest of honor. It was typical of lavished, spoiled Mexican youth, and he was just a pawn in the whole affair.

He was not here because he was a bullfighter. Of course, it made it easier and more subtle, but it was about last on the reasons for the sudden invitation, and Guy cursed Marcos for being such a fool. They would be laughing at him, the moment he left. He was the jester in the princess' court, and right now he was doing a slow burn.

It all made sense, too much sense, and the food choked in Guy's throat. He wanted to spit it out on the table, and stalk out of the room, but that would be playing into their hands. Apparently, Vita had a crush on him, a girl's crush like American girls did on Rock Hudson, but Vita's family was in a position to show her that her idol had very clay feet. They could crook their little finger, and bullfight managers all over Mexico would stumble over each other, doing the beck and bid of Don San Benito. It was exactly as he figured; only now that he knew, he decided to play a game all his own; a game called "Make the Virgin."

He felt a hand touch his arm, and turned to face Dona Beatrice. "Is something wrong, Senor? Your face —"

He looked at her levelly, "There is nothing wrong with *me,* Dona."

She caught his accent, lifting an eyebrow, "You imply — Senor, do you understand Spanish?"

"Perfectament bien," Guy said flatly.

She paled, "Senor, it was a little foolish — no, it was very foolish for us to do this." She tightened her grip on his arm, "Senor, I will pay you well to leave now.

"Immediately after this meal, I pay you two hundred and fifty thousand pesos," she said quietly. "I will give it to you —"

"That is a lot of money," Guy commented.

"I am a wealthy woman," she said. "I tried to tell them that it would not work."

"This won't work either, Dona Beatrice," he smiled, "I'm staying, and you're being very quiet about everything. If you tell a soul, even Don San Benito that I know his little game, I'll go a lot farther than you ever dreamed possible."

"How, Sen —" Her voice trailed off, as she looked across the table to Vita, who was smiling at Guy. Clearly, both of them understood exactly what he could do, and Vita would go along willingly. The old lady's eyes shifted to Eduardo, weak and worthless, and then back to Vita. Vita's husband would take over the San Benito ganaderia, because Eduardo was a fool, and Don San Benito was a fool, but old Dona Beatrice was not a fool.

She saw the look which passed between Vita and Guy, and she began a struggle within herself. The man would never hurt her granddaughter, and she knew it with absolute certainty. He was not a coward she knew that; she had read and re-read Vita's collection of press clippings about El Oro, and if there was any-thing about his record, it was that Guy was not a coward.

Neither was he Vita's kind of man.

Dona Beatrice had seen her family grow and expand, and degenerate, until Eduardo was the male heir apparent, and deep inside herself, Dona Beatrice loathed her grandson. It would have been better if Eduardo was half as much man as the bullfighter.

She nodded, watching them, and Guy was unaware of the change in her expression. She forced distaste to form wrinkles around her mouth and sharpen her lips; she withdrew her hand from his arm "Very well, torero, you win, this time. But, remem-ber, I would die before I saw her hurt."

"It might serve you well, to remember your own words," Guy flung it in her face, and it was all Dona Beatrice could do to con-tain herself. It had been years and years since there was such a man at the ganaderia de San Benito. She looked at Vita with a flash of envy; if Dona Beatrice had been fifty years younger and their ages more approximate, Vita San Benito would have had to fight for the torero.

That was for sure. But, Dona Beatrice was an actress, and she had opposed Don Juan's little game of romantic musical chairs, from the beginning. To pull a switch now might upset things, and it might be the last thing in her life which Dona Beatrice would genuinely enjoy, but she wanted to follow this romance.

She even wanted to mix in it a little.

Of course, she was old and had old fashioned ideas, but then she also knew how to be careful, very careful, especially around men. It was an art which her generation of Mexican ladies learned well, and as far as Dona Beatrice was concerned the blatant affairs of Eduardo were like the vulgar taste of cheap, green beer.

Dinner was over, followed by coffee and cigars in the living room, and Guy noticed that Eduardo had disappeared, as had Quiqui. Marcos came in with Guy, and seemed entirely pleased by the affair, and Guy did not have the heart to tell him that it was all a monstrous joke. As they left the living room, Guy watched Vita leave with Dona Beatrice, and went to his own room with Marcos walking beside him. Marcos was excited about the tentadero in the morning. The horses and caballeros were already gathered, and the bulls were herded into nearby pastures, separated from the cows, and the calves were ready to be put to the test.

It would be good, Marcos kept insisting, and was puzzled when Guy did not respond. He left Marcos at his door, begging off with the conversation, using the excuse that he was tired after the long trip and the night before had been no easy game.

Marcos was still befuddled, as Guy closed his door between them—and faced Alice Kantrell.

"Bienvenidos, torero," she smiled, rising from a heavy chair where she had been enthroned.

"I thought this was my room," Guy said.

"One door down," she pointed to the next room.

"I'm sorry," Guy turned to leave, when she grabbed his arm. "What's the big hurry? I was coming over there anyway. I thought we might talk about Texas; you know, all that old 'wave the Lone Star flag' jazz."

Guy laughed, "They'd hang you by your thumbs from the ceiling of the Alamo."

"It's about all that hasn't happened to me," Alice grinned. "Are you familiar with San Antonio?"

"I was there in the Army," Gus said. "I know where all the whorehouses are."

She smiled, "Is that where you found Marge?"

"Hardly," he shrugged, "I picked her up in Breckenridge Park."

"Oh-h-h-h!" She groaned playfully, "All those familiar names and places! It makes me want to cry. Can I use your shoulder?"

"Be my guest," Guy said, "How about us sitting while we're at it?"

"Goody! You aren't in a hurry," she swished across the room, lifting her arms to him. For the first time, Guy noticed that Alice was wearing a thin, flowing negligee, with nothing, or next to nothing under it. She tilted her head, "May I kiss you? I always like to kiss men hello."

"Hello," Guy grinned, "But is Eduardo somewhere in the shadows?"

"Eduardo?"

"I thought you two were a pair," Guy said.

"Only when it suits us," she came against Guy, lifting her lips to him. "Now kiss me, or I'll start singing *The Eyes of Texas Are Upon You,* and I can't sing worth a damn."

"I'll bet you're good at other things," Guy commented.

"Try me!"

He did, and for a Dallas gal, she really knew how to put the ooooomph! into her kisses.

It did not start out like a kiss hunting new frontiers, but it abruptly changed course, and Guy suddenly felt the tiredness leave his body, creeping out — and vigor took its place. He clamped his hands on her waist, and pulled her tight against him, pressing her hard enough that he could feel the peak of her breasts, even through his shirt. They felt big and warm, like soft cushions, and if a guy had to sleep in a great big house like this, there was no better place to start than nuzzled between large, firm breasts.

He did not want it to come too fast; he was in no mood for experiments tonight, but he wanted to tease her a little. After all, if it wasn't worth a struggle, it was hardly worth the bother.

He separated their lips by a good two inches, and the nipple of her breast still scratched his shirt, and he could feel every contour of her hips and thighs, gently rubbing against his leg and abdomen.

"That was a nice hello kiss," she crooned.

"Let's relax a little," Guy said. "Tell me about Texas."

"Oh, let's drop Texas!" she exclaimed.

"All of it?"

Her lower lip was pouting, when suddenly she had to laugh, and it was as good reason as any to fall back in Guy's arms.

"Maybe not all of it," she said, "But I've had a fling at most of it."

"Must have kept you busy," Guy commented drily, "all those oil field workers and cowboys."

She reached up and touched his nose with the tip of her finger, "I like bullfighters, myself. How about you?"

"I like girls."

"Then, I'm in luck," she grinned. "Not everybody around here appreciates a good girl." Pressing her hand into Guy's, Alice led him across the room, past the bed and to the fireplace. The flames crackled low, and as Guy watched she dropped a twisted mesquite root into the coals. It sputtered as Guy slipped behind her circling her waist with his arms. Pulling her tight against him, Guy felt her round soft buttocks cushion and yield to the angular hardness of his hips. His hands began to explore her body, skimming over the smooth fabric of her negligee, he touched the rise of her ribs and pushing upward, he nudged the ball of his hand against the soft swell of her breasts.

She arched her neck, laying her head against his shoulder and Guy nuzzled his lips against her ear, and breathing softly, he traced its ridges with tongue tip lightness. He felt her shiver against him, and draw his arms tighter, then with her fingers she cupped his hands and filled them with her fullness.

He felt the red nipples against his palms and began to knead them, closing his hands and opening his grip with persuasive rhythm.

"You know, for strangers," Guy whispered softly, "we get along real good."

She grinned, cooing softly, "We're not strangers. I knew we'd do this the first time I saw you. That's why I wanted this room."

"You planned this?"

"Not really," she turned in his arms, "I just wanted every-thing ideally situated so that it could happen. Are you angry?"

"Of course not," Guy said, as Alice's fingers began to loosen the buttons of his shirt rapidly. She tugged until the shirt was free of his slacks, then stripped it from his shoulders and tossed it on the chair. When she turned back to him, Guy saw candid admiration in her eyes, and was glad that his physique was good enough to make her look at him that way. "You like what you see?"

"I liked it when I first saw it in the bull ring," she said. "That's the thing about the way matadors dress; there is very little left for a girl to imagine."

She stepped nearer, running her hands over the naked skin of his chest and waist; stretching her arms to circle his shoulders, she brushed her cheek against his body. Then, she closed her lips and pressed them in a moist kiss on each of his male nipples. Slowly she opened her lips, and began to circle them with her tongue, and it had a startling effect on Guy. He knew they were not worth a damn for most things, about the most useless things a man had, but with her doing this to him, well, it was sensational.

She raised her head, leaving a red trail across his chest, and lifted her face to take Guy's kiss. He came down over her; her mouth yielded and Guy aggressed against her, driving into the red warmth of her lips. His tongue flicked the ridge of her teeth, and their tongues met in a passionate ritual of roughness and smoothness, touching, caressing and darting, probing deeper and deeper, and then with languid ease drawing away, as Guy began to strip off the filmy thin negligee.

It felt very soft, and very feminine, as he crumpled it in his hand, drawing it off her until Alice stood bare and splendidly naked in front of him. Her back was to him for an instant, and Guy looked with savor at the white plains and valleys of her back, the plunge of her backbone, which rose in identical, sensual cheeks of flawlessly white flesh.

She made him stand erect, as she stripped away his tight slacks and her hands explored his body in the quick nervous way of a woman who is about to take what she has wanted for a long time.

"I want you naked too," she said, and Guy obliged her, dropping the last of his clothes on the carpet. Then, she took his hand, and sinking down on the soft rug, lifted her arms to him. "Love me here, in front of the fire."

All the lights were off, and only the orangish glow of the flames reflected off their bodies, as she yielded her arms to Guy, bring his lips to cover her mouth with a demanding, seeking kiss, which drove deeper and deeper into her, unfurling all the passions of her body, and creating an even more intense desire to satisfy her lusts with him.

She stretched out on the carpet, and Guy took one of her breasts in each of his hands; butting the nipples into his palm, he began to repeat the rhythm he'd done before. In the firelight, her flesh seemed to glow, and the tight pressure of his fingers made her swell, and she groaned with ecstatic pleasure. "Keep doing that, squeeze them harder, it feels so good. You don't know how good it feels to have you do that. You've got such big strong hands, keep doing it!"

She seemed to twist and writhe beneath him, but he formed a different grip on her breasts, circling them and forcing the hard nipple through the circle of his thumb and forefinger. Then, when it stood hard and perfect, he flicked across each with his tongue, and Alice became a wanton creature of pure passion.

With her hands behind his neck, she pressed his lips harder and harder against the nipples, and Guy drew them into his lips, covering them with warmth and gently nipping them with his teeth.

"Oh Guy!" She groaned, "I knew it would be like this. I knew it the first time I saw you — you're wonderful — just keep doing it! It makes me feel like I've drunk acid and everything inside me is burning up! I love it!"

And, she did.

Guy lifted his kiss, tracing the lines of her throat, pressing his chest hard against the softer flesh of her breasts. He eased himself up, up, and Alice squirmed under him, arranging herself to make room for his body. He wanted it to be slow and complete, as he eased past the last barriers and drove deeper and deeper.

Deeper.

She made low gutteral sounds in the back of her throat, arching her hips to meet the full hilt plunge of his body; clinging to him, Alice swooped and drove against him with fierce determination.

And it went on and on.

Guy would have slowed it, but Alice's body seemed to drive against him, butting her flesh in a jolting rhythm which made slowness impossible for Guy.

She drove harder.

Harder.

Faster and faster.

Guy felt as if he were caught up in a whip whirlwind that threatened to suck out his insides. It got worse and worse, beautifully worse, and he thought that when it happened, he would lose everything.

She swooped, meeting the thrust of his body, and driving them closer and closer to the peak.

Closer.

Then with awesome suddenness, they stood on the brink of the explosion, and then with throbbing pulsation it ripped through them, starting in Guy's body and dying in the deepest part of her.

Slowly the fire died.

They clung together, body to body, and then Guy raised on one elbow, "That was nice."

She chuckled, "For a starter."

"There's more?"

She laughed now, "Not tonight, matador." She glanced up to a clock on the mantel. "You've got to hurry."

"Why?"

"We're having a party tonight and Eduardo is coming to get me. I've got to take a rapid bath, and you've got to get out of here. You know how Latins are, jealous and all."

"You mean you're going to sleep with Eduardo tonight, after what we just did?" Guy asked, and almost expected the vexed expression on her face.

"Do you think that you're the only person in my life?" She was trying to be flippant, "Good Heavens! A girl can do it every fifteen minutes, and enjoy it."

"That's why you were in a hurry," Guy said.

She came over beside him, "Matador, you're fun in bed. I like sex, and the first time I saw you in that skin-tight Suit of Lights, I knew I was going to have you. I want you again, but right now, I've got to go to a party."

"What kind of party?"

"Don't be silly," she said. "A sex party, of course."

"Here?" Guy asked, incredulous.

She sighed, "Any time you get this many men and women together, you can drum up a party. It might not be the perfect group, but at least it beats sleeping."

"Well, I'm going to try sleeping."

"Don't bet on it," she grinned. "Someone just might decide to come sleep with you."

"You're disgusting," Guy said, beginning to dress. It sounded like a joke to Alice, and she chuckled at it, but it was not mirthful to Guy. He dressed quickly, and left without thanking her, because he figured that he was just the first in a chain tonight for Alice. Hell, he might not even be the first with a goddamn nymphomaniac like her. If this was part of "sophisticated sex," Guy was beginning to tire of it already.

It was no good for a man's pride, his ego, or anything to be simply the first in a long series of sex partners. In order to join in with this little "fun" group, Guy reasoned that a man would have to surrender all his pride. He would have to be a groveling sensation seeker, living from one erotic climax to another, with practically nothing in between.

It was sex, raw and simple sex, with nothing else involved, not so much emotion as one of them would show for their pet fish.

It was sensual and vulgar, and somehow Guy felt degraded by it. Still, he was no damn preacher, nor any. St. George out to kill all the dragons; he was a man, and he liked a good bang too. But, there should be more to it than just whim-wham, thank-you-M'am.

At least, the couples should be on friendly terms.

Apparently, a gal like Alice would shack up with anything — just for kicks — and from what she said, he was the desirable novelty around here.

With that thought in mind, Guy locked the door of his room, took a complete shower, and slipped between the sheets exhausted and nude. With the door locked, he would get a reasonable night's rest, and with it open, no telling who he would wake up in bed with. It might even be Eduardo, and then he would have to bash his face in, and that would put the quietus on anything between him and Vita.

Vita.

He almost grinned as he thought of her, and the entourage around the family princess. Well, he was going to turn out to be one birthday present the princess would never forget. That was for sure.

CHAPTER TEN

GUY WAS AWAKE OF MOTION around him, as he woke.
It was the sound of the shutters opening that first roused him, then he realized that there was someone in the room with him, *and* he had locked the door.

He sat bolt upright, flinging back the sheet, his feet landing flat on the floor.

"All right! Who is it?" he shouted, groggily shaking the sleep out of his eyes.

Then he saw her; Vita.

Almost in panic, he snatched the sheet to cover his nakedness, and made it, but not quite before she had turned to face him.

"It's the day of the tentadero," she smiled. "You look very nice when you're asleep. Your man, Paco, could not get in the room to wake you, so I opened the door for him. Are you mad?"

"No, just naked," Guy said. "Now get out, so I can get dressed."

She walked over to him, and with a sudden flash of brazenness, she lifted his chin and kissed him. "Good morning, Torero."

"You better watch out," Guy warned playfully. "I always feel best when I've had a good night's sleep, and right now I feel like ending a chapter in your life."

She laughed lightly, "Hurry, Guy, I'm holding breakfast for you." With that, she whisked across the room, and swirled out the door in a flurry of bright colors.

If it was the way they awoke around here, Guy thoroughly approved. In fact, there were quite a few things of which he approved at Ganaderia San Benito, and quite a few things which he intended to change — like the little game El Don and the matriarch La Dona Beatrice were playing with him, but that could wait. Right now, he savored the chance to have a little time with Vita, alone. Or, would this be another San Benito banquet?

Paco was up to the fiesta of the tentadero, and he had laid out Guy's clothes for the day, with the same care he kept for the bullfighting regalia — with good reason. Though the tentadero was not a full-fledged fight, it was still a matter of coming face to face with an animal bred to kill men. The young bulls would not be fought, but the heifers were killers too; in fact the point of the tentadero was to judge which of them were the bravest.

For today, Guy would wear black trousers, so tight that if he had possessed a single ounce of flab, it would have rolled around the waist. His shirt was Spanish, heavily ruffled with full long sleeves, with ruffles and lace on the cuffs. He knew in the United States such a shirt would have been the butt of a joke, but here it was a status symbol, a badge of his profession, and he was proud to wear it. He wore high, black boots of smooth, shining leather. His small jacket hid most of the shirt's ornamentation, and snugged against his body almost as tightly as the trousers, but hung open to the waist. At his neck, he wore a black shoestring tie, and topped the whole outfit with a wide brimmed Caballero's hat, tied under his chin at a jaunty angle with black cord and held snug by a turquoise clasp.

When he was finished, he looked in the mirror and approved. He was dressed for the fight, and even Paco was pleased. It was an important day; he was the honor guest of the tentadero of San Benito ganaderia; no matter what intrigue brought him here, the press and reporters would be at the pits, and he would be performing for them. It would be the smallest crowd before which Guy had ever appeared, but perhaps the most important. He knew that not just the heifers were being tested for bravery today.

He dropped the hat on a hall table, as he started toward the dining room. Vita met him in the hall.

"Aiyee! Matador," she smiled, "You are even more handsome this way than in your Suit of Lights."

"I'm a hungry matador, right now," Guy teased, "Is the San Benito Council of War waiting for us?"

She laughed, circling her arm in his, "For today, we are alone."

Guy nodded, "That, I will like very much."

She guided him down a smaller hall, then through French doors onto a tiny enclosed patio. The wall must have been eight feet high, and the shrubbery was lush and thick, but like he was beginning to feel about most things around here, Guy did not trust appearances.

He was right not to, because through a small window. deftly hidden by iron grillework, which was equally obscured with bright-red, climbing roses, La Dona Beatrice watched her granddaughter have breakfast with the American matador. She watched unashamed, and when they were nearly finished, she closed a small iron door, and turned to her daughter. "He did not touch her."

"Do you think — well, that he's like Eduardo?" The younger Senora stammered out the question which had not come between them, until right now.

The old woman stood rigid, her back like a black-iron poker, and her eyes fairly flashed at her daughter-in-law. "You are a fool! I am surrounded by fools! If he is like Eduardo, then why did he spend the time with that American woman? She told me that he was very much of a man."

"You sent her there?" Dona San Benito looked at her husband's mother with amazement.

"Of course, you idiot!" She snapped. "Do you think I want Vita to marry a man like her brother? Now let's go to the bulls."

"What if he — " Vita's mother almost choked on the thought, but she finally blurted it out. "What if he has ideas of sleeping with Vita?"

The old woman looked at her with scorn, "What man with two healthy genitals wouldn't?"

"What about her virginity?" Senora San Benito gasped.

"My dear," the old woman's tone changed to patience, "She's going to lose it someday, please God, or she'll be a lonely old maid."

"Jesumaria!" Vita's mother crossed herself, and followed the grand old lady of the San Benito family out of the small, dark room, the only purpose of which was to spy on the intimate little patio, where Guy and Vita were finishing breakfast.

"Is this your first tentadero, Guy?" Vita asked.

"Yes, and I hope it is good," he said.

She came close, and because she knew it was safe now the window was closed, she kissed him. It was a mixed kiss, and a kiss which Guy found difficult to understand, but easy to respond to. There was the sweet tenderness, but now there a hint of eagerness in Vita's lips. The taste of her was fresh and young, and as she clung to him, Guy suddenly realized that Vita was probably the only virgin whom he had kissed in his entire life.

"Buena suerte," she whispered softly.

"Do you mean it?" He asked sincerely.

"With all my heart, Matador," she pecked his lips again. Then, holding herself very tight against Guy's chest, "I love you."

"Don't be crazy, I'm not the right guy for you," he said brusquely, trying to hide the fact that all at once, it was a good sound. He had the feeling of a maverick colt who, in spite of his wobbly legs, jumps and cavorts while playing in wide-open green fields.

"Right or wrong, it's the truth," Vita said softly, "I love you. Papa thought if I met you, I would find out that you were insolent and I would forget you, and find a husband my family would choose. But I love you."

"You know, I've got a wife," Guy said, and for the first time, he had a reason to get rid of Marge, a real reason, not just some manufactured fear of adverse publicity. He wanted this girl in his arms, he wanted her, and he knew that it was impossible.

"Just kiss me now," she sighed. "Just for now, let's not talk about problems."

He did, and it was the most wonderful thing, which had ever happened to Guy Moran.

He fell in love.

It was impossible and crazy, upside-down, and there were knots that could never be worked out, but he loved her, and he felt younger than young, happier than happy, and when he went to fight in the tentadero, he was splendid.

El Don San Benito had expected the American torero to be good, but he had not bargained for what he witnessed. It turned him into one of El Oro's most ardent fans.

The tentadero was just the final act of a long week of preparation. First, the ganaderia's caballeros rounded up the thousands of head of cattle belonging to El Don Then, with a milling herd on hand, they began to separate them, the bulls returning to pasture, the cows and calves into a separate section.

After this, the cows, which were the most dangerous of all, because they had fought men, were driven from their calves. The calves were separated by sex, males into one waiting pen, the females into another.

Last evening, the best males had been picked for the tentadero. This judging was by appearance only, the rejected ones being shipped to the slaughterhouse. The females went through a similar process, so that this morning only the best were waiting for the test of bravery.

A huge "V" wall ended in the square calf ring. It was unlike a regular bull ring, with eight-foot adobe and concrete walls. The "V" opened into the ring with a torile, and to each side of this door was a small section of seats for reporters, critics, employees and members of the San Benito family. Below this section was a small room for the becerristas, who made a profession of fighting calves. With them were several carefully chosen novilleros, and his old friend Tacon was obvious by his absence. On very special occasions, such as this, a full-fledged Matador was present, and his was the place of prestige.

"Bienvenido, maestro," the youngest of the two novilleros saluted Guy as he came into the room prepared for the fighters. He was just a kid, hardly eighteen, and very new at this business. Ordinarily, Guy would have kept to himself, but the boy was obviously nervous and Guy's fame did nothing to put him at ease.

"What's bothering you, torero?" Guy used the term deliberately, inferring that the boy was a torero. The kid smiled.

"It's my first tentadero, maestro," he said.

Guy laughed, "Don't be nervous about that; it's my first one, also."

"De veras, maestro?" The boy looked surprised.

"Nothing could be truer," Guy said. "Just pray that the heifers don't kill us. If we can keep them from catching us, we'll be all right."

"Buena suerte, maestro," the boy was a little straighter now, and taller. He had a lot of filling out to do, before he could strike a handsome profile in the ring, but there was promise, lots of promise, and all his life he could remember the day he fought at a tentadero with El Oro.

Only part of his cuadrilla had come with Guy. He chose Paco to handle the swords, just in case they were needed, but usually they did not kill in a tentadero. Pablo would do the inciting for this, and only Macon had also come, though picadors would not be used. The most important was Pablo, and Guy watched him carefully, as he brought the first heifer in for her first charge at the cape.

"Huh! Huh!" Pablo growled, whipping the cape so that she charged hard and straight, and Pablo dove for protection. He was grinning from ear to ear as he dusted his trousers and turned to Guy.

"She is a good one, maestro."

"Be careful, mi matador," Marcos brushed Guy's shoulder affectionately, "Remember that heifers can kill also."

"Right," Guy said, and stepped into the center of the calf ring. Everyone had been waiting for this, through two performances by the novilleros, and now they were as alert as if they were watching a murder unfold.

"Vaa-aaca!" Guy called her, drooping the cerise capote in a gentle sweep over the sand. "Venga Vaca!" With a flip of his wrist, Guy snapped the corner of the capote, and she lunged toward him, her sides heaving in the hot sun, her brute instinct driving her to plunge her horn in the man's soft belly.

Guy pulled her to the right, drawing her within a breath of his stomach, and her hair whisked across the shirt's stiff ruffles. They heard the sound in the stands, and they were on their feet, cheering.

He brought her back for a second, then a third charge, using his full cape; he incited her to lunge harder and harder as he executed one brilliant turn after another.

The heifer was dazed as Guy turned his back on her, and walked out of the calf-ring, ignoring the gasp in the stands and the hoarse bursts of the calf's breath.

"Maestro!" Marcos exclaimed, "Don't turn your back on a female She will charge your back!"

"That heifer was not going to charge again," Guy said confidently. "When I left her, she could not see three feet in front of her."

"Maestro, that is so dangerous," Marcos said. "Be more careful."

Guy looked up at the stands, "See that old woman up there, La Dona Beatrice?"

"Si, maestro," Marcos nodded.

"When she stands up and cheers, for me," Guy said firmly, "The tentadero will be over."

"For God's sake, maestro," Marcos grabbed his arm, "Don't take any chances for an old woman!"

"It's not *for* her, Marcos," Guy said. "Not really."

During the next round of calves, the young novillero took a minor gore, which did little to hurt him but spilled blood in the calf ring. The boy handled himself with courage and there was a look of sheer pride in his face when Guy joined the others in a round of applause for his work. It was nothing spectacular, all of them knew it, but it took a lot of guts for the kid to stay there after his leg had been ripped. It was the novillero's first corona, and each injury afterward would only be painful, but this one was his initiation into the brotherhood, and he wore it like a badge of honor.

When Pablo took Guy's final calf through the initial capework, he ducked behind the fence and grabbed Guy's arm. "Burriciego, maestro!" *Burriciego* meant just one thing, and perhaps under other circumstances, Guy would not have fought the farsighted cow. Still, his afternoon had not been what he wanted, though it had been good in every way. *Burriciego* meant that the cow could not see well at close distances, and would not respond to the cape like a cow with good sight. It made it doubly dangerous, and the spectators sensed something wrong. A whisper went through the small gathering, and Guy saw Don San Benito leave his seat and start in this direction.

He would not let him stop his fight.

Quickly, Guy stepped into the ring, "Vaa-ah-ca! Ole!" He whipped the capote in front of him, the cow whirling with her nose lifted, tail twitching the air.

"Ole!" He clipped, "Ole!"

She bellowed, pawing, and roared toward Guy like black fury. Now, he had to depend on her instincts, because she could not be diverted by the capework. He brought her in for the first classic veronica, and when he glanced up, the crowd was hushed and waiting. The second veronica whirled her around him, and then he brought her back. Everything was going right with the cow, she worked good, though Guy knew that she could not see; slowly he was gaining the upper hand on her, as he stepped in front of her, holding his capote like limp, flowing fluid.

"Vaa-a-ca! Venga!" He whisked the capote in front of him, but she started backing away, sniffing the air and sand. She was going to take a *querencia,* a stance from which she would not budge, and she was taking it where the young novillero had taken his gore.

A burriciego in a querencia.

It was the worst possible situation, and everyone knew it. Guy tried cape work to pull her out, but the cow was having none of it. Quickly, he stepped behind the fence, "Paco! My sword!"

Guy took it, and the capote, and stalked to the cow. She bellowed, pawing, but not breaking into a charge; the closer Guy came, the wilder her grunts, and when she still balked at cape work, he took the sword from its sheath.

Aiming carefully, he swatted her with the flat of the sword across the tip of her nose. A wild bellow of rage ripped from her, as she bolted from the querencia, and took a stand to charge from across the ring.

Guy was quick, bringing her charge away from the querencia; the rest of his passes were perfect, and when it was over even La Dona Beatrice stood to applaud.

"Bueno, Matador," the old woman said later as they left the ring for the house, "But, would it not have been easier to send her out to pasture? Why should you be so careless of yourself?"

Shrugging, Guy looked her in the eye, "The easy way to kill bulls is in the slaughterhouses, Senora."

"You are right, Matador." she smiled, "very right."

Over her shoulder, he saw Vita coming toward them, running so that her jet hair fanned and bounced behind her. Touching his hat. he bowed to her, "Excuse me, there is someone I want to meet again."

The old woman's eyes narrowed, "Like I warned you, Matador, be careful with my granddaughter."

"Dona Beatrice," he exaggerated his words, holding out the soft pronunciation with just a hint of mockery. "I would die before I caused pain to a woman who loves me."

"Senor—!" she exclaimed, but it was too late. Her eyes followed him, and the old woman saw her granddaughter throw herself into Guy's arms, and kiss him wildly as a reaction to the nearness of his death with the cow.

CHAPTER ELEVEN

THE ONLY TROUBLE WITH VITA being in love with Guy, and his using it to teach the San Benito family to quit interfering with her — and that he belonged to no one, not even the richest ganaderia in Mexico,— was that Guy found himself in a reaction he'd never felt before. It was strangely akin to love; in fact it was love for Vita, but he had to find a way to handle it.

Love was not a simple thing for Guy.

Instead, it was extremely complicated, considering there was Bambi waiting in Agua Caliente — but a big check would take care of her. There was Marge, also waiting in Agua Caliente. Marge might be downright unappreciative of her husband's falling in love with a dark-eyed, dark-haired Mexican girl. Not that Marge objected to the emotional part of it, and Guy knew that she did not give two flips who he shacked with; but dear old Marge had staked a claim on his earnings, and was she ever going to scream when that claim was threatened.

He used the dirt and dust of the calf ring for a chance to be alone, and to sort out what he felt about this affair. He had to make some determination about what he was going to do about Vita.

He chided himself as he undressed and slipped into a heavy terry-cloth robe. He was ten years her senior, and what she felt for him was just a girl's crush. He was a fool to think that he loved her and she loved him. Great Hannah, he had never even been to bed with her!

While he bathed, he resolved that it would have to stop. They both needed a chance to know one another, to get their bearings and by that time Vita would have forgotten him. Then, as he considered that possibility, Guy knew that he did not want Vita to forget him. Just the opposite, he wanted her to remember him all her life, and he wanted it to be right with her, because when they were married —

Marriage to Vita!

It went through Guy's brain like a white-hot poker, and it seemed almost so ridiculous that he had to laugh aloud to himself, as he came into his room to dress.

"What is so amusing, Matador?"

"Dona Beatrice!" Guy pulled his robe tighter around him, "You shouldn't have come into my room."

"And, why, Matador?" she asked.

"Hell! A man might as well leave the door open," Guy commented. "This is like a railroad station."

"Do you think, Matador, that at my age, you have anything I haven't seen before?" She spread her graceful hands on her lap, "I came to talk to you, Senor, about my granddaughter."

Guy sank on the bed, lighting a cigarette, "Talk,"

"She is in love with you," she commented.

"I know that," Guy blew a cloud of blue gray smoke into the air. "What else?"

The old woman's voice was as clear as a bell, "Senor Guy, she is very dear to her family; she is the last hope of a long proud line."

"There's Edu —"

She stopped him, raising her hand, palm out, "Senor Guy, I am here not to play word games with you; I know about my grandson, and I do not approve of him. I love him, but I don't like what he does. He is not a man."

"What about Vita?"

She leaned toward him, and as Guy watched her, he realized that she was a very old woman. There was something so old and so tired in her eyes, that for a moment Guy forgot where he was. "How do you feel about her?"

Guy shifted uneasily, "It's too soon really; I think that I could —"

"Senor!" Her hand slapped the arm of her chair with a crack. "I told you, please, no word games. You know how you feel. I know how you feel, but I must hear it from your lips. I must know what you intend to do about it!"

Guy stood up, stalked to the window, drew deep on his cigarette, and when he turned he was frowning. "Senora, I had no intention of this happening. Last night, when I realized that El Don had brought me here as sort of a birthday present, I thought I'd make her fall in love with me, then I'd —" She wanted it straight on the line, so he gave it to her, "I'd make love to her, and leave her. I wanted to see if all this wealth could repair a virgin's shattered maidenhead."

"Do you still feel that way, Senor Guy?" she asked.

Guy sighed audibly, "No."

"How do you feel, Senor?" she demanded.

"I am in love with your granddaughter," he said plainly. "I don't know what I'm going to do about it; I don't know what I *can* do about it, but I do love her." He walked to her, "I can promise you this, Dona Beatrice, I won't hurt her. If there is any way I can keep from doing it, I won't hurt her."

She rose carefully, "Thank you, Senor, that is all I wanted to know." Guy watched as she crossed the room, her old back to him, still holding the erect carriage of centuries of breeding and culture. Her step was sure, and Gay noticed that even now, after so many years, her grooming was immaculate. She reached the door and placed her hand on the knob, then she turned back to him. "By the way, El Oro, today you were magnificent at the tentadero."

Before he could answer her, she was gone, and he knew that it was right this way. If he had been confused about how he felt for Vita, Dona Beatrice had crystalized his ideas now. Somehow, there had to be a right answer — somewhere, there had to be a way for him and the girl he loved.

Marcos left that evening for Tacquil, and took the remainder of the cuadrilla with him. He would have to attend the meetings in preparation for the fight, draw lots for Guy's bulls, and see to it that there were accommodations at the local hotels. The other members of the cuadrilla were anxious to get there, because their families were waiting. For the first time in his life, Guy began to understand the drive of a man to be with the woman he loved.

And, for the first time in his life, he shared the intimacy of a family. It was like walking into a brightly lit room from the street, and Guy did not know what Dona Beatrice had decided, but there was a dramatic change in the family's treatment of him.

There was an almost hushed expectancy when he came to the living room after dinner, with Vita on his arm. She was flushed and happy, and when they came into the room, Guy heard one of her female cousins titter, giggling in the corner.

It was his first time to face the family, assembled for the evening together. It was an hour of shifting from one side of his chair to the other, looking desperately for an ashtray, which Vita provided by using an antique glass cup, which brought a gasp from another female cousin. When she sat down beside him, the cousins waited breathlessly for the axe to fall, but it did not, and Guy saw the faintest hint of a smile on Don Beatrice's lips.

He was in! He was in with the old matriarch, and she was the real power here. He did not know for sure why, but he wasn't going to question it, any more than he did when Don San Benito handed him the keys to a car and suggested that they take a drive.

"We have some beautiful scenery in this part of Mexico, Don Guy," he said. "Why don't you and Vita go for a drive?" Guy was the first to catch the use of the title of respect, Don. He did not know from where it came, from the fight, or from the old lady, but it was his now, and used by Don San Benito himself. It was practically a carte blanche; he could write his own ticket from here in, with the family. There were reservations, of course; what had been given could be taken away, and Guy knew it.

But, Don San Benito was right about one thing, the scenery was exhilarating. The car was a middle-priced American convertible, and with top down, Vita pointed out the road winding up into the mountains. In the daytime, the land before them stretched parched, and dry, but now it was dark and full of shadows. It looked cool, and lonely cacti stood like giant fingers through the earth's sandy crust.

"It's very beautiful," Guy said.

"I've seen it many times," Vita said, laying her head against his shoulder, feeling the warm strength of his arm circled over her back. "The stars are bright."

"You're very beautiful," Guy whispered.

She looked up, through almost closed eyes. "I don't ever want to hear that from any other man."

"I better not catch any other man saying it to you."

"You love me?" she whispered.

"Do you have to ask?" He brushed her face with his hand, "Don't you know?"

"Yes," she sighed, "But, I like to hear it."

"I love you," he said, "A thousand, million times, I love you."

Then, he kissed her, and it was all that their first kiss had been, and more. It was the sun and moon, whirling in one mass of eternity and dipping down to scatter joy all over him. Her lips were sweeter than anything he had ever touched to his, and he let their kiss linger, their lips clinging moistly together, and their breath mingling in the cool of the dark night air.

"Querido!" she cried, "Love me."

"I can't," Guy pulled away. "Don't you understand? it has to be right for us This wouldn't be right. It would be like kids, sneaking kisses in a car. When I make love to you, I want it to be perfect."

"No one would ever know," she said.

"I would know," Guy said honestly, "And, for some crazy, silly reason, it's very important. It's never been this way before; I've never felt like this, but this is important. You've got to know what everything is about."

"Something bothers you, querido?"

"I've got to tell you about my wife," Guy said flatly.

"Does she love you?" Vita asked.

"No," Guy said, "I don't suppose she ever did, and it's a long, involved story how it all happened. I was a soldier, and it was sort of a shotgun wedding."

"Do you love her?" Vita asked.

"Of course not," Guy said abruptly. "I love you."

"That's all that's important, querido." She pressed her hands to his cheeks; lifting herself, she kissed him again. She held it, and Guy opened his mind and body to her. Vita became the aggressor, the probing huntress, driving her tongue between his lips, and pressing her body against his.

Then, Guy held her close and stroked her hair, "We'd better stop now, while we can."

"Whatever you want, querido," she said.

He looked down into her eyes, "You know I want to make love to you, but I can't, not yet. At least, not until I'm sure of where we're going, and what we're going to do."

"I love you," she nuzzled against him.

"Will you come to Tacquil with me?" he asked, and saw her face cloud. "I want you to be there."

"I would hate the bulls," she said frankly. "I would be afraid. I could not stand to see you fight again. I would die myself, if anything happened."

"Did you know that for the first time since I started this thing, there'll be someone there who really gives a damn whether the bull's horns get me or not?"

Guy was beginning to understand a lot of things.

"Didn't your wife care?" Vita asked, surprised.

"She cared," he said, "but in her own words, the reason she cared was because the bull did not pay her bills."

Vita sat up erect, "What kind of woman is she? She must be a strange wife."

"We haven't been husband and wife for years," Guy said, and he knew that it was true, but he did not want to bring Marge here, even by mentioning her name. He touched his finger to her lips. "Will you come to Tacquil?"

"Nothing could stop me from being with you; not even the bulls," she said, "because I love you."

And she did, and he did, and they sealed it with their lips pressed together, barely able to contain the passion which sprang between them.

From that moment on, Guy Moran was alive.

CHAPTER TWELVE

Saturday afternoon, Guy left for Tacquil in a small sports car which Marcos had rented and left at the ganaderia for him to use. He drove with the top down, in spite of the sun, and arrived in Tacquil with a red flush of sunburn.

"By God!" Marcos threw his arms around Guy, "Going to San Benito was the best idea I have ever had. You look ten years younger."

"I feel it, amigo," Guy slapped his shoulder. "What's going on in this place, anyway?"

"Aiyee, dioses!" Marcos cried, "This is a terrible town. The hotel is old, the church is falling down, the houses have no windows, but they know about you, El Oro. They know you are here, and every seat in the plaza has been sold." He winked, "And, there are pretty girls, even in Tacquil."

"Forget it, amigo," Guy said heading toward his room.

"Bambi is not here," Marcos said, "And, neither is Marge. Maybe I should send you some company. You know how you are before a fight."

"It won't start until in the morning," Guy said flatly, and they both knew he was talking about the fear. It would not come tonight, because he went out to the fiesta or found a bar full of *aficionados,* who kept his glass full and toasted him with each new round of tequila.

Vita had changed Guy, but not even Vita could drive away the fear. Tequila helped the night before, and Guy was too restless to stay in his room. Marcos was out on the town, the entire cuadrilla was gone; he was alone in the hotel when he finished dinner and decided to take a walk on the street.

Of course, Guy was not really alone, no famous man is, but he was just a little more than surprised, when he saw Eduardo and Quiqui coming across the street toward him. Even if Eduardo was Vita's brother, Guy would have given him the old heave-ho, but he was Quiqui's friend, and for his sake, he did not oust Eduardo.

"We came early," Quiqui said. "How about some tequila?"

"You staying here?"

"Aiyee!" Eduardo said, "There is no other place in this miserable town."

"Amigo, we have three bottles of good tequila, a bag of lemons and a sack of salt," Quiqui nudged him. "What do you say we make a night of it?"

"Where's Alice Kantrell?" Guy asked. "I thought she'd be with you, Eduardo."

He laughed, and Guy noticed a shrill note to it, "No. She's back at the ranch, shacked up with that novillero who got the little gore in the tentadero. You know Alice; she likes it different every night." He winked at Guy, "She's tells me that you're quite a man."

"Not here, Eduardo," Quiqui stopped him, just before Guy gave in to an urge to hit his good-looking face. "Let's go upstairs. You got a room, amigo?"

"Sure. Want to go there?" Guy said.

"It'd be best; all they had left when we got here was the damn broom closet," Quiqui said. "You're popular, amigo; the peones are coming into this town like ants after honey."

Quiqui was right about one thing. Tacquil was packed, but most of the peones in town could not afford a hotel room. Through their window, Guy heard them on the streets; it was a babble of noise and of cantina music. Guy listened as Quiqui and Eduardo seemed to drink the tequila with a vengeance, taking it straight, drink after drink. Quiqui was sprawled on a small couch with Eduardo beside him, and the tequila on the table in front of them. He watched Guy grow more and more restless the longer they drank.

"It's a bad night to be alone, right, amigo?" He grinned, "Maybe you should find some company."

Guy turned from the window, "This is the worst night of all, the night before a fight."

"Here," Eduardo held up the bottle, "Drink a little. We know what it is to be lonely, eh Quiqui? Ahh, but you bullfighters are lucky. You get rich, and then you die. Look at us!" He hit his chest with an empty thud, "We're born rich, but who cares? The women don't follow us, or pray for us—they just want us to buy them. We just stay rich and rot; the women we buy are like Alice. Last night she was with you, tonight she is with the novillero. What kind of life is that, torero?"

"Maybe you'd like to be poor," Quiqui grinned, slapping his cousin's leg. "I'd rather be rich and rotten, than poor and pure."

"Qui sas." Eduardo leaned over and put his face in the couch cushion, still holding to the tequila bottle. Quiqui looked at him sadly, then turned to Guy. "No one except maybe me understands Eduardo. If he had any guts he'd be a great reformer. Aiyee! But we talk a lot, and drink a lot, and you do nothing. What eats you, amigo? Are you sad for Vita?"

"It's this way before every fight," Guy mused, "I think I'll try the tequila."

As the hours passed and the tequila supply dwindled, Guy decided that Quiqui was right — it was hell to be alone like this. He listened for the street noises, but they were dying. He needed someone, and Quiqui and Eduardo had fallen asleep on the couch. He needed company; he considered leaving the room, but then he thought about Vita and decided that this time he would stick it out without a Bambi. So, he stripped and burrowed into bed; at least the tequila helped here. Sleep came with difficulty. At last, it came, but only in snatches.

It was almost morning when Guy woke to the strange noises of passion. For a moment, it was too unfamiliar for him to get his bearings, but then he realized that the sounds were coming from the couch where Quiqui and Eduardo were sleeping. Darkness had given way to the gray haze of early morning, and he could make out the shapes of their bodies clinging together. He felt a wave of complete revulsion. He had thought that Eduardo was bad, but he had never associated what he was with Quiqui. In a way, it made sense, but what they were doing was insane.

His first impulse was to bound from bed, and heave them from his room, but he was as if he were hypnotized. They were two classically handsome Mexicans, the early sun caught on their dark skins, glowing with the softness of gold. Any one of a thousand women would have loved them, but they sought their orgy together, groaning and sighing, clinging to one another, and the heat of their passions and lusts sent shudders through their body.

Guy watched with horror.

Still, he was fascinated and curious, as they drove one another higher and higher, and then a little wail broke from one of their lips, and ended with a sobbing jerk as they clutched their bodies together, trembling at the peak of their passion.

Guy buried his face.

It was bad. bad, very bad for him.

And, today was the day of the fight.

He rose from bed, not caring that they heard him and knew that he had witnessed their orgy. He snatched up his clothes and dressed, bolting from the room as if frightened of what he had seen.

Marcos, an early riser was genuinely surprised to see Guy up at this dawn hour. "Maestro, what's wrong?"

Guy pointed back to his room, "There are two people in my room. Get them out! Keep them out!"

"Bueno, maestro," Marcos said quickly, "But you...?"

"I'm going out," Guy turned on his heel and stalked away from his friend. Marcos knew him well enough so that he understood Guy wanted this time to be alone. It had happened before, the first time that Guy found out about Marge, but never on the morning of a corrida. It disturbed Marcos, who followed him at a discreet distance, until Guy stepped onto the street. Then, Marcos turned back to the room. It would be clear, when his torero returned.

Guy walked almost aimlessly, but a sense of direction turned him toward the plaza de toros. It was empty now, as he climbed to the top of the bleachers, and looked down at the sandy circle where he would face three bulls this afternoon. A paper whipped across the surface, rolling, empty and meaningless, and it seemed to have something to say. Guy watched, sitting with his elbows resting on his knees and watching the white scrap of paper.

Some people were like that piece of paper, going nowhere and doing nothing. For the first time in his life he asked himself if he had any more meaning than that paper. When a bull finally got him — and the odds were that one would; they killed even the greatest matadors, and Guy was not proud enough to consider himself as great — what would they say about him? Lover? A great sex partner? A lousy husband? A good torero; perhaps the best American matador?

He left the ring without finding any answers. He cut beneath the stands and into the bull pens. There were nine of them; big, black bulls from the ganaderia San Benito. He rested his arms on the top rail, and watched them, milling together. In less than an hour, Marcos and the other managers would meet here, and draw lots for his bulls and the other fighters' bulls. One of the others was a young boy, just making his way into the profession; a novillero in the real sense of the word.

There were eighteen horns, ready to kill them.

They looked deadly.

They were lethal.

"You bastards," Guy muttered, and one of the bulls looked up at the sound of his voice. "You black, mean bastards." He knew they did not understand, and even if they could, a bull could care less what his enemy thought of him. Bulls were born to kill matadors. This afternoon three of them would have their fling at him, but at least they were doing what was natural, and that was more than Guy could say for a lot of people he knew.

Marcos did not like Guy's mood. It had been this way all day, and now that the fight was nearer, it did not change. He should have insisted that Bambi come; sometimes when she left his room Guy was exhausted, but at least there was not this atmosphere of depression. His torero could laugh at him, could make a joke about Paco's virginity and slap Bambi's tail.

Even the Suit of Lights was wrong; they brought him the light blue with silver and crystal. He looked very handsome, but Marcos was disturbed. "Maestro," he hedged, then blurted out his suggestion, something they had never done in the length of Guy's career. "Maestro, we could cancel out, saying you're sick. Others do it."

Guy picked up his cape; a wide, heavy white satin affair with a crust of silver thread and crystals, designed in light blue roses. It was a beautiful *traje des luces,* but it did not match Guy's mood.

He felt black inside.

Marcos was firmly convinced that it was going to be a terrible day. The car struggled through the street mob, the women screaming and throwing flowers, the little boys racing after them, some crouching on the back bumper.

They shouted his name, but today Guy ignored them.

"Maestro—" Marcos started.

"I'll fight, Marcos," Guy said, clipping his word, then he closed his eyes.

It was bad; very, very bad for Marcos. His stomach felt burning and hot, and there was an unhappy knot in his throat. He had heard Guy with *La Macarena* right before they left the room today, and he asked Her for something different. He asked less than that the bulls did not catch him; he asked that the bulls not *kill* him. Guy's choice of words caused Marcos' mental anguish.

They worked their way into the inner patio where the fight officials, some of the cuadrillas and the aficionados waited in little clusters. Some saluted Guy, a couple shook his hand, but most of them respected the torero's desire to be alone right now. Guy lit a cigarette, and looked toward the gate to the ring, when a hand touched his arm. He whirled, "Vita, I didn't think you'd be able to make it. I looked for you this morning."

"I am here, Guy," she smiled.

He looked at her, and she was even more beautiful than he remembered. Her dress was ivory brocade silk, tight and snug around her breasts and waist, but flaring and full over her hips to her knees. She wore her hair high, and studded with a tiny clip, which Guy supposed was real diamonds, but over it all, the classic long veil of black lace, which draped soft and beautiful, like the sigh of wind in a church.

He knew that all the people in the patio were watching them, and for her to be here was almost brazen. If she was here, in the holy of holies for bullfighters, and she was for him, then — well, there was just one speculation. Vita San Benito and El Oro were lovers.

"May I kiss you?" he asked.

"If you didn't, I would be disappointed."

Guy did not want to disappoint her, so he held her close and through the silk brocade, Vita felt the silver and crystal crust of his Suit of Lights.

"Cuidado, Amor," she whispered, "Please, please be careful."

"You won't see the fight?" Guy asked.

"No," she sighed, "I'll be where the women who love bull-fighters belong."

Oh, God! It was important — never had it been important before, but today it was, somehow — that a woman who loved him should be in the chapel.

He looked younger, felt better and the depressive air and mood were all gone, as Vita left him and went into the tiny chapel of *La Macarena,* where the Aves would match the intensity of the crowd's cheers.

Marcos saw it, sighed, and the burning in his stomach stopped. It was almost as if they had all been held up by weak timbers, and now a firm footing was there. The tension was gone, and it was almost a physical relief which went over Guy's cuadrilla.

"Let's go," Guy told them, "It is going to be a very good day."

CHAPTER THIRTEEN

I T WAS A GOOD DAY. Because of his stature and popularity, he took the first bull to burst through the toriles. It was a tall bull, with broad black shoulders, a massive hunk of pawing, huffing fury.

Guy stood behind the burladero, as the bull whirled at the sound of the crowd. The arena was packed and loud. The bull raised its tail; digging into the sand, it bellowed low and long.

"Listen to him," Marcos stood beside Guy. "He is a big one."

"Let's see how he works," he signaled Pablo, who scampered into the ring, flipping his capote to attract the bull and draw him through a charge.

The bull grunted, lowered his head and roared at Pablo, who stepped back and let him pass. The bull's sides heaved, glistening in the sun with sweat as he whirled and came at the peon again.

Pablo vaulted the fence, dropping to his feet near Guy, "He is a good bull, maestro; he charges straight."

That was all Guy needed.

It was his show now.

Guy was perfection, executing each pass with ease and grace, his feet never budging, no matter how close the bull zipped past him. He brought it closer and closer, and the fans were on their feet shouting, cheering with each execution.

Then he killed.

He sank the sword to its hilt on the first try, the bull dropping in its tracks with a final grunt.

The stands almost turned into a mob.

Holding his montera high, he circled the ring once, and they cheered on and on. He circled again, and the women threw flowers and wept in the stands.

He was their torero.

The first novillero's fight was clumsy, and the crowd seemed to be sitting on its hands for him. Guy felt sorry for the boy, who wanted so badly to please them he was taking crazy risks. His kill was bad; four tries before the bull died. Some clapped and some booed as the boy came behind the burladero. Guy tried to console him, but the boy whirled at him with anger in his face.

The third fight was no better, worse if anything, and when Guy's second bull charged into the ring, they were on their feet shouting even before Guy stepped into the ring.

They had come to see and cheer El Oro.

And, they cheered wildly through his second fight, awarding him the ears and tail, shouting as he circled the ring three times, montera up high into the air, and pesos fluttered down like colored confetti.

It had a bad effect on the young novilleros.

Guy saw it coming after his third fight, which was like a crown. The crowd began to thin, even with two more bulls, and the boy seemed to be intent on outdoing him. Guy knew how he felt; he had been a novillero once, and fought for a crumb of the cheers, but the boy was taking chances, even more now than earlier.

Guy by rights could leave the ring after his third bull, but he stayed, smoking a cigarette and watching the boy fight, in the callejon. He was right in figuring that if he remained the crowd would stay, and the boy caught their attention with a very good pass.

They cheered him.

He brought the bull in again, this time closer.

Too close and the crowd screamed.

It went into the air like the shrill cry of a banshee, as they saw the bull's horn sink into the boy's groin. He held him pinioned for a moment, up in the air, and then with a thrust of his head, he tossed the novillero into the air. Blood spurted out on the sand, and the boy lay like a heap of crumpled satin.

Guy sprang to his feet.

The boys peones were there, but too excited to keep the bull from charging the boy's body. It lunged, sinking in its horn again, nudging the boy with its massive, slick nose.

Guy came in fast; flashing and whipping his cape in front of him, he took a stand in the center of the ring. "Toro! Ahh-h-h! Toro!"

The bull turned, blood dripping from his horn.

It took only minutes for the boy to be carried to the infirmary, but even before he killed the boy's bull, Guy knew the novillero was dead.

The people in the stands were tense and silent, shocked as they realized a boy was dead. There was a pool of blood where his body had fallen, and now Guy stood over the killer, sprawled in a black mound at his feet.

Ordinarily he would have walked away from a dead bull, but everything seemed to be snowballing on him now. The hushed people waited, the only sounds were from a woman, probably the boy's mother or sister, or even his lover screaming hysterically as they carried his body away.

Guy's feet were planted wide apart, his legs straight, and he held his muleta cape in his right hand, hanging limp, and it was as though everything was somewhere else, waiting for what he would do. He was completely alone, just him and the dead killer. Its nose, black and wet, aimed at his right foot; the banderilleras hung still now, the last spasms of the bull's body not even jerking them. His sword protruded from the bull's shoulders in a glistening pool of bright red blood.

Guy's life flashed in front of his eyes.

This bull could easily have been *his* killer.

Someday, a bull would have that honor.

The great horn curving up from the bull's head was dark with a boy's blood, and it could have been his own blood.

With an almost military turn, Guy walked out of the ring, and he would never be the same again.

There were changes he wanted to make in his life, things he wanted to do, and he knew that he was going to have to live with one of his mistakes; Marge.

She was his wife.

He was in love with Vita, but he could not ask her to take him as he was. The situation was impossible, and it could not go on as it was.

She was waiting in the patio, and went to the hotel with him. It had to be now; he brushed away the masseur whom Marcos had hired, and hustled all the others away from him, until they were alone.

He walked away from her, and looked at the tiny statue of *La Macarena*. She could hear his words, "Thank you, they did not kill me, today."

She waited, sensing that they had reached a crossroads; she could not help but admire the lithe movement of his body as he took away the heavy jacket, tossing it on the bed. He turned, "I'm going to bathe. Will you wait."

"Always, Amor," she said, and he flinched.

"Please, don't love me," Guy said, "It will be easier."

"You are frightened?" She lifted her hand to him.

"I am always afraid of the bulls," Guy said. "But, it is different now."

"My father wants you to quit fighting," she said quickly. "He asked me to offer you the job of manager of the ganaderia. Please, take it, Guy!"

He studied her face with a new twist inside him, which seemed to wrench and shake everything in him. Gently, he reached and touched her cheeks; his fingertips smoothed her eyes and he touched her lips. She felt the flutter in his hand. She looked up, "What is it, Guy?"

"You know I love you?" he asked.

"And, I love you," she said quickly, ready to come into his arms, but he stopped her.

"The hardest thing I have ever done in my life, is right now," Guy said, pressing his hands to his face. "It has to stop between us Vita, now."

"Guy —!"

"Please!" He turned, but she jumped to her feet, pressing herself against him.

"You don't mean it!"

"Great God!" he said, "I do mean it. It must stop, while it can. If we go any farther, I'll make love to you. I want it more than anything — but —"

She lifted her hands to his cheeks, turning his face to her, "I want it too, Amor. I want you to love me."

"We can never marry," he warned. "You can't even come with me when I fight —"

She pulled herself up, pressing her lips to his to stop his flow of words and warnings which she did not want to hear. "Love me, Guy. please love me!"

He reached for her pressing her tight against him, his lips found hers and crushed them, and she opened her lips to him offering him the last sacred secrets of her body. His mind whirled with a madness that demanded they satisfy this need between them, and when he broke his kiss, he felt strange and unembarrassed before her.

His body was hot and dirty from the ring, and he would not go to bed this way with her. Still, as he shed the satin trousers and ruffled shirt, he was still unashamed. She looked on from a seat by the window, her legs drawn up under her, and Guy saw her admiration for him in her face. She seemed to glow, and he was glad that he had this body, and this woman who wanted his body. He wanted her to take all of him, as he would take her, and somehow he knew that it would be right and perfect.

"Un momento, querida," he pecked her lips.

She clung to him, "Hurry."

And, he did.

When he finished, Guy came back to the bedroom, not really knowing if the embarrassment which had been lacking before would spring between them. His eyes widened in surprise as he saw her, waiting nude and like a virginal nymph in her bed. She lifted her arms to him, and he came toward her quickly.

"Amor!" she cried, as he stretched her back on the bed, her hair spraying out like a mass of glistening black silk; his lips found hers again, and held as his hands began to explore the pure flawlessness of her body.

Her breasts were large and firm, and young. He touched her, and then as if shocked by what he did, drew his hand away. She took his hand in hers, and put it back until it butted against the mounded swell of flesh, which was crested with a dark nipple like a jewel.

"Do you like me?" she said. "I like you."

"You're beautiful," Guy said, sweeping his hand down to her waist and finding the little lines of her abdomen. He pressed his fingers into the contours of her belly. Spreading his palm, he covered the rise of her stomach, then followed the long "V" line of her legs.

With his other hand, he stroked her back, diving deeper and deeper, until he cupped her perfect round buttocks in his palms; he drew her body against him, as he pressed his lips against her breasts, suckling as if he would take love from her body as he would give love to her heart, and she whimpered like a little kitten just before she purred against him.

"Now," she sighed, and yielded to the harder, taut flesh of his body.

For a moment, Guy hesitated, because he knew that it would hurt her, and Vita sensed his reluctance to cause her pain. With a sudden sweep of her hips, she drove against the motion of his body, and the barrier of her virginity split. Even though she wanted it, and welcomed it, she could not stifle a partial cry of pain as her body seemed to recoil with heat and hurt.

He stroked her cheeks and fondled her breast, "I didn't want to hurt you. I love you."

"It is the only hurt I've ever liked," she cooed softly, running her fingers through his hair. "Oh, Guy! It is wonderful."

And it was; it was the perfection of his body, lean and hard, muscular and in its way a symphony of masculinity, driving into the softer, feminine body which hungered to take all of him into her, to caress and fondle him with all the secret part of her. Where her gentle body was soft and mounded, he angled with bone and muscle, and it was beautiful and right; it was perfect.

She took the rhythm of his love, the slow drive as he eased deeper and harder against her, and she made it her rhythm, and it mated with the pounding of their blood. Their lips held; their tongues met stroke for stroke, they caressed and clung, mounting up and up.

Higher.

More perfect than the first perfection.

She wept, butting against him, crying as he held her, and he knew that it was not from pain now, but from happiness. And he was happy. Very happy. He felt as tall as the sky, and rich as the earth and as endless as the sea. He gave her all of himself, and she yielded the last particle of her body to him, crooning the sweet low dove's call at mating, and she felt the swoop of a gull inside, the dizzy exhilaration of being where she had never been before. She held on to him as if she would lose consciousness if she were away, even a fraction of an inch. She cherished the full consciousness of what they were doing, and she longed to know him more and more.

More and up. Higher. Up.

And, then, as though there were nothing else, no higher place, they stood together on the brink of forever. They tangled their bodies, their hands, their lips and lives, and then they plunged to the exhaustion of perfect passion.

The world heaved under them.

The sky tilted.

The stars trembled and hovered over them.

It was over and it was beautiful.

She stroked his face with her hand, "I love you. All my life, I knew this would happen to me. I love you. I'm so glad that it is you who took my first love."

"I was not a virgin," Guy said, regretting it.

"It is different with a man," she smiled. "I knew, and I'm not sorry. Are you sorry?"

"Not that I loved you," Guy confessed. "Nothing has ever made me happier than this. It complicates things for us; we've got to find a way. I can't live without you."

She went wild, kissing him with little kisses all over his face, his throat and his body. She touched her lips to his stomach; as if she wanted to make the last possible tribute, she then touched her lips to him.

It was an offering, as sacred and beautiful as the meaning of what they had just shared. Suddenly, Guy knew that in a way, he was virginal to her. She had taken a part of him which he had not known existed, but by taking it, she left him whole. It was a contradiction—a magnificent, erotic contradiction, and he felt happy all over.

CHAPTER FOURTEEN

I T HAPPENED IN AGUA CALIENTE.

The bull caught him. Guy knew it was going to happen

Nothing had gone right since he left Vita in San Benito, where it was like leaving part of himself. He refused to let her join the entourage of campfollowers, prostitutes and thrill-hungry women, who were as much a part of bullfighting as the *aficionados,* or the bulls, themselves.

He knew that Vita was no match for Marge, and dear old Marge was there to meet his car when he arrived at the hotel. As before, she was the gushing wife, for the photographers, and besides, she was beginning to be bored with Agua Caliente. It was a big town, but a gal like Marge can go through even a big town in three weeks.

On top of it all, she was running short of cash.

Marge went through a bankroll, like she did men: with a sense of grim determination.

It did not do her pride a bit of good for Guy to refuse to see her alone before the fight, and he kept himself away from her even the next morning. He slept late that day, and when he woke, took a long steam bath; a heavy-set man gave him a complete rub down, and when it was over Marcos signaled for the barber who dipped his hair and shaved him.

Agua Caliente was an important town, and the crowd would be used to good bullfighters. He had a billing with two full-fledged matadors, and it was shaping up as a good day.

Paco laid out his rose suit; the only other one ready was the blue, and it had been too close to death for Guy to wear it yet.

At noon, Marcos returned from the ring with the report on the bulls. They looked good, a little large, but not too badly colored. They had heard that the Agua Caliente ring owner was in trouble financially, and cutting corners. Marcos had been especially careful in his inspection, and there was nothing concrete to prove that the man had bought second-best bulls.

As was his custom, Guy took a light lunch; he ate steak, lean and rare, a tossed salad with vinegar dressing and black coffee. No more.

At one o'clock, he began to dress.

Paco had bought new silk stockings to match the rose suit, and the pants had been repaired of a small scratch from the last time Guy wore it. It was made of smooth rose silk encrusted with gold embroidery, a wide band of elaborate decoration down both sides to the tight legs just below his knees.

Marcos checked the tassels carefully, and Jose helped him put on the chaquetilla. He took his dress cape, a wide resplendent affair of brocade and gold, designed in an intricate floral pattern.

He picked up his black montera and turned to his friends, "Vamanos!"

It turned out to be a very bad day.

The crowd was demanding, and the bulls were second class. Guy knew that something was wrong with his first bull from the moment Pablo took it through the initial capework. It was a very, very dangerous bull with a bad hook to the right. But Guy worked it beautifully. He brought it through a veronica, holding the cape low, and inciting it with a low hoarse rumble. "Toro!"

It did not charge good, or straight, and capework was impossible.

He killed it, after gaining permission, and he killed it honestly, but the crowd barely applauded.

"They didn't like me," he told Marcos.

"Maybe the next one will be better, maestro," he said, but it was not.

It was of the same caliber, and demanded an equally quick turn at the sword. When his third and last bull of the day came out, even the crowd could see that this was the worst of the three.

But it was his last chance.

"You're not going to do well with this one," Marcos pointed to the huge animal, standing in the center of the ring, wagging his horns in the air. "Kill it quick. The fans will be here another time."

"Double him for me, Pablo," Guy ignored Marcos, and the bull hardly doubled at all. He resisted Pablo's calls and ignored the cape.

"Kill him quick," Marcos pleaded.

"Let me see what I can do," Guy said. "They want to see me fight."

"To Hell with them!" Marcos cried.

"My capote," he held out his hand, and Jose placed a new purple-red capote in his hand. Quickly he stepped from behind the burladero, "To-r-rro!"

He walked toward the bull, spread the cape and drew it through a full veronica. Then, turning, he drew it back, trying to get it close to his stomach, but the bull refused to make a good charge. He tried another veronica, and another, then he tried a natural, but the bull was not charging right.

The trumpet pealed, and the picadores came out.

The bull lunged at the horses, catching Macon off guard as he sank his horns into the padding and began to lunge against the horse. Macon flailed his arms, and spilled out on the sand.

The bull whirled, stepped back lowering its head, a grumbling bellow erupting from its throat. The picador lay helpless against the bull's charge.

Guy was quick.

He snatched his capote, and bolted into the ring. He flung it, snapping the cloth loudly, "Toro! Toro! Ah-h-h-h! Toro!"

The bull turned to meet the challenge, and the picador scrambled over the fence to safety. Guy pulled him through a veronica, snapping the cape high and over his shoulder. The bull lunged at the cape, all four feet drawn up, its horns on perfect target with a fatal gore to the right. Guy brought it through again, and the crowd began to cheer, and he pulled it into another charge.

Then, he came to the fence for his sword and muleta.

"Matador," Marcos said, "Kill it for God's sake."

"Not yet, Marcos," he smiled. "Not quite now."

He began the last act, his cuadrilla crowded into the ring, hovering at the edge. They knew that this bull was dangerous, more dangerous than ever, but Guy would fight him. Their matador might need them. Guy ordered them out of the ring, "I will do it alone."

And he did.

Holding his arms straight, he brought the bull in for a terrifying Pass of Death, which had the stands screaming.

Then through another Pass of Death.

He followed with the low sweep derechazo, then holding the cape in front of him, he drew the huge animal against his body in a sweeping natural. The bull grunted, twisting and following the cape as if it were part of the fabric, and Guy was in complete control.

Guy stood statuesque, not budging an inch as he brought it in for another. And another.

And another.

They shrilled his name, shouting and stomping.

Clapping.

"El Oro! El Oro!"

Then it was the time to kill. Guy drew the bull toward his body slowly, holding the sword poised in his right hand, sweeping the muleta with his left.

The sword found its mark, deep and blood gushed from bulls neck, as he hooked wildly to the left.

Guy's teeth clenched, and his eyes burned wildly as he felt the horn sink into his leg. He looked and he was high above the bull's back. People were screaming and his cuadrilla was running into the ring.

"Guy!" Marcos leaped the fence, but it was too late.

He flew up, spinning and then everything went black as he hit the ground.

It seemed hours later that he regained consciousness in the Agua Caliente hospital. When he woke, there were flowers from Bambi in Mexico City. She heard his injury on the radio, and she was sorry that she was not in Agua Caliente, but she was sure he would understand.

Goodbye Bambi, Guy mused.

Three weeks in Agua Caliente was too much

A nun hovered nearby, and when she realized Guy was awake she signaled for the doctor, who plunged a syringe into his arm, and sleep came back.

It was four days before they would allow him to regain consciousness, and then the pain from the corona was almost unbearable. It swept over him in hot red flashes, and he screamed, begging to die.

Only, he was not going to die. He was feeling the pain now, and that was the best sign for a torero. He would live and he would go back into the ring, and he knew it. Only he would break into a sweat when he thought of facing another bull. Cold fear began to creep over him, and Marge did nothing to help.

She came to the hospital twice, neatly timing it so that reporters saw her tears, and almost did not notice the young Tacon comforting the weeping woman.

Guy saw the picture in the paper, and he was sick another way.

He refused to see anyone, except Marcos.

His manager stayed beside him almost all the time, trying in one way or another to make it easier, but that was almost impossible, because Guy had two hurts: the corona, which was bad enough, but he also hurt inside.

Marcos waited for him to mention Vita's name, but he did not. Guy was thinking about himself and the women in his life, and the bulls. There was plenty of money for him to retire now. Plenty. It might look like he was running, but — was it that he wanted to run? He began to question his own courage, and he was not the only one. Three days later, Marge got past everyone in spite of the doctor's orders that she was not to see him. Guy understood how, knowing just what kind of scene Marge could create on a moment's notice.

"How long are you going to be here?" she asked.

"Why?"

"I just wanted to know if you were going to fight any more this season," she said. "I already talked to Marcos about the money I'll be needing."

"Marge," Guy looked up at her, caught her hand and pulled her to his bed, "I want to know something. Do you think there is any chance for our marriage?"

"What a hellava question," she arched her eyebrow. "Are you thinking about trying to get out?"

"I may be," Guy said, "but on the other hand I might be thinking of us going back to the States, and us giving it a try."

"Are you nuts?" she snapped. "What would you do in the States? You're a bullfighter, and it's illegal in the States. If you think I'm going to sit out on another goddamn ranch, you're nuts."

"Marge, it might be our last chance," he said.

She laughed, "Oh Honey! If you think I'm going to divorce you, you've got one more thought coming. I'm hanging on, and if you want to be crucified in the papers, just you start a divorce from me. I'll make you look worse than Bluebeard, I'll wash all our dirty linen on the main plaza, and drum up a crowd."

"Skip it," Guy said, turning away from her. "Why don't you go to Mexico City?"

"Who is she, lover boy?" Marge demanded.

"Who?"

"The 'who' who has you thinking about divorce," Marge stamped her foot angrily, "That's who! Who is she? It is not that idiot Bambi, I know. Where did you meet her? In Tacquil?"

"None of your goddamn business," Guy hissed, "And if you don't get out of here, I'll call Marcos. Nothing on earth would give him more pleasure than to throw your rear downstairs. Now, get!"

"You swine!" she snapped, "I'm not through with you yet. I'll find out who she is, and when I get through she'll be worse than a rag doll."

"Get out!"

"You bastard!"

"You heard me," Guy pushed himself up on his elbow, "Get!"

She did, slamming the door behind her, and Marcos across the hall winced at the loud noise. She stopped, staring at Marcos, before she stomped over to him, without any try at acting the lady.

"Who is the bitch he is in love with?" she hissed.

"Him, in love?" Marcos shrugged.

"You goddamn spick!" she hissed, "You know who she is. Tell me!"

"I don't know, and if I did, I would not tell."

She lifted her arm, as if to bring her bag crashing down on his head, but Marcos was quicker. "Look, reporters!"

It worked, and by the time she realized there were no reporters, Marcos was gone, but not into Guy's room. He did not come there for another thirty minutes, and in his shirt pocket was the carbon of a telegram, which naturally he did not show Guy.

Guy never learned about the telegram, not even on the day Vita arrived. It took two days to drive from San Benito, and El Don came with her. When Marcos met her in front of the hospital, her eyes were swollen and red, and she was completely unaware of the people around her. "How is he?"

Marcos beamed, "He'll be a lot better in about five minutes."

"I want to go to him alone," she said.

"I wouldn't have it any other way," he agreed, winking to El Don who stayed behind her. "Room 414."

"Gracias," she kissed his cheek and bolted from them. Marcos wondered if she were going to wait for the elevator, but it was his job now, to stall Marge and El Don San Benito.

"Senor," El Don came up to him, "Does he love my daughter?"

"Never in his life has he ever loved anyone like he loves her."

"Not even his wife?"

"Especially not her, Don San Benito," Marcos said, then slipping his hand under the worried man's elbow he turned them toward a small cafe. "It's a long story; come, El Don, I will tell you all about my matador."

CHAPTER FIFTEEN

GUY LAY IN BED, ALMOST INERT. He heard the door open and presumed that it was Marcos, or one of the hospital sisters. He did not open his eyes, or turn his head in the direction of the footsteps.

Then, he felt her lips touch his. His eyes flew open. It had better not be Marcos kissing him, or one of the nuns.

It was Vita, and he threw his arms around her, kissing her frantically.

"You came!" He repeated it again to himself.

"Of course, as soon as I could," she said, "And, now we are going back to San Benito, just you and me. Papa is there, but Dona Beatrice told me that if you argued, I should clobber you with a flowerpot. Maybe this one."

She reached for the vase holding Bambi's goodbye flowers, and Guy calculated that it would be singularly appropriate.

"My mother taught me never to argue with beautiful women," Guy said quickly, "I must say she was right."

Vita laughed, "How do you feel, Amor?"

"Never better," Guy teased, "I just might get up and fight a bull tomorrow."

She shook her head, "I guess I'll have to clobber you yet. If you feel so good, we'll leave right away for San Benito."

"Not until I've kissed you."

"I've been waiting."

"Never keep a lady waiting," Guy said.

"Another of your mother's sayings?" Vita asked.

"Ummhuh," Guy nodded.

"Act instead of talk, Amor —"

He did, and she loved it.

Their position was very compromising, if a nun should have walked in the door. Vita was pressed against his hand as it cupped her hard breast and began to squeeze, his arms circling her and his fingers gently kneading the flesh of her shoulders.

She skimmed his face and throat with her lips, lingering deliciously on his lips, and then tracing the line of his lips with her tongue. "We've got to get you out of here, or —"

"Shall we go now?" Guy teased.

"Kiss me," and it was no joke, and he did not try to make it into one. He held her tighter and tighter, and she rested her head in the curve of his shoulder, as he cupped her other breast, too, and began to squeeze her rhythmically. She giggled softly, "Be careful, you'll start something you can't finish."

"Coronas make it hard for lovers," he said.

"There are ways," she said. "I've been thinking about us all the way here, and they have an ambulance waiting to take us to San Benito."

"Well, do tell!" They whirled to see Marge standing in the door. "If this isn't a cozy scene."

"Go home, Marge," Guy said.

"I'm his wife," she sneered at Vita. "I don't suppose you happen to be a nurse or anything logical like that."

Vita was too shocked to answer; she began trying to straighten her dress and hair, and Marge moved in. This was the way she liked the odds, all in her favor. "So you think you're going to get my husband, you little slut!"

"Marge!" Guy shoved up on one elbow.

"Let me tell you something, you dirty little witch," she threw her hand back toward Guy, "He's a bastard. He'll screw anything that'll get in bed with him, ask anyone. Ask the other girls he's all told he'd marry, sweetie! He can't marry anyone. He's already married to lil' ole me, and I'm not getting off this gravy train for you or anyone else."

Guy was sitting up, ready to force himself from bed, when the door opened again, and an indignant Sister appeared with a uniformed militiaman. She pointed to Marge, "It's her, officer. She barged into the hospital, and came here in spite of doctor's orders. I warned her."

The policeman grabbed Marge's elbow, "Come on."

"You sonavabitch!" she shrilled, hitting him with her bag. "Who called you? He's my husband!"

Vita had sunk into a chair shaking, and the Sister closed her eyes, as if that would stop Marge's verbal filth and even her presence.

The last Guy saw of her, Marge was still swinging her bag at the policeman. The Sister crossed herself as she closed the door, "Now, Senor Moran, the doctor has released you to Don San Benito, and the ambulance is ready and waiting. It was an honor to have you in our hospital; you are a fine matador."

Guy knew that it was not the last they'd hear of dear old Marge, but for awhile it was enough. She was one problem which did not have to be faced, at least for the time being.

The ambulance ride was smooth, and when they eased him into his familiar bed at San Benito, he already felt better. Nursing nuns might be absolute marvels, but Vita was a miracle. Within two weeks, the corona was healed, and Guy hobbled out of his room to eat with the family. There was no occasion now, and it was a pleasant, intimate meal.

"To all the happy times at San Benito," she said, lifting her glass, and Guy joined it readily.

He did not know how long he would be here, but he had been very sick. Now he was better, but still exhausted, so he skipped the after dinner coffee and cigars.

Vita helped him to his room, undressed him and put him in bed. Then, to his surprise, she stripped and eased her body between his sheets, nuzzling up against him.

It was very good medicine.

Excellent medicine, in fact.

She made him lie stretched on his back, and she became the aggressive one now. She let him hold her in his strong arms, and his lips set the tempo of their sex. Then, she hovered over his body with her own, and Guy's hands rested on her sweeping hips, and he guided her down to cover him.

It was superb medicine.

She eased over him, arching her neck and back, she let her hair fall free, swinging in the dim light of the bedroom. Soft sounds filled the room, whispers of love and lust and sex, and she drove on and on.

She went farther.

Farther.

And, when it happened, it was a shuddering, sweeping sensation which erupted from the very deepest part of his body and flooded her with the emotions and warmth of his feeling for her.

Then, she cuddled in his arms, and laying her cheek on his shoulder, she slept like a child, but Guy lay awake wondering what Marge was going to do. It was impossible that she would do nothing; he knew her too well to even hope for that. She would try to destroy Vita, and she had no scruples about how she did it.

If he won anything from Marge, it would be very expensive. He tried to calculate what her price would be. Would she settle for the money they had? He doubted it, because when it came to money, Marge was like an adding machine already totalling next year's income.

When her next move did come, four days later, it came through Tacon, and it came as a complete surprise. At breakfast, Guy opened *La Prensa* to see his picture next to Tacon's:

"NOVILLERO CHALLENGES AMERICAN TORERO TO *MANO A MANO.*"

Tacon was demanding a face to face showdown.

It seemed completely unfair, but beautifully timed.

Tacon had everything to gain and nothing to lose.

He knew that Guy could not fight now.

But, he would look like a coward if he delayed, and every moment of delay would make it worse. It took the newspapers about two hours to dig up where he was staying, and the San Benito phone began ringing.

He refused all calls.

Still, he knew that it would only take them a few more hours to have reporters at the ganaderia, and then what would he do? His very first move was to contact Marcos, who was so angry that he sputtered. At every mention of Tacon's name, Marcos cursed him. "That dirty, cheeky bastard!"

Guy tried to calm him, "Marcos, Marge is behind this. Can't you see that?"

"She's a witch, a bitch, a heat-crazed female dog," he said, "That's what she is."

"I agree," Guy said patiently, "but what are we going to do."

"Sit tight," Marcos said finally. "Let me see how the thing is shaping up here, and I'll drive up right away. How is the leg?"

"Better," Guy answered.

"Good," Marcos said, "you know, we may have to accept this little snip's challenge. He's trying to make you out a coward."

"I'll leave that to you," Guy said, looking to Vita, who was pacing the floor. She was unalterably opposed to this; she knew that the corona was only surfaced, not healed, and she was less worried about what they thought about her man, than she was about the man himself.

It was very nice for Guy to know she cared, but it did nothing to make things easier for him. In fact, it only complicated it for her to act as if every time he took a step he was going to break open the wound. She practically screamed at her father when he agreed to allow Guy to practice in the tentadero pens, with San Benito bulls. And, Vita practically wailed out her anger and frustration that evening, when Guy told her that he intended to go into the pit and try a bull the next morning.

"No! No!" she shouted, "Your leg is not well!"

"Vita!" Dona Beatrice was on her feet, slapping the table beside. "You knew what he was, when you fell in love with him. He is a bullfighter, and he must fight bulls with courage. You are a bullfighter's woman, your place is to love him, not to try and decide his future. His future is already determined."

"Grandmama!" Vita gasped, but it was the last of her vocal opposition. She did a very good job of opposing it in other ways; that night she did not come to Guy, and he spent most of the night hours flexing his legs, trying to overcome the pain which shot down from where the bull had sunk his horn into his leg.

It still hurt the next morning when Guy dressed in tight trousers, a white shirt and a wide brimmed hat to protect his eyes from the sun. It was aching when he stepped into the ring, and the torile gate swung open.

The bull was small and black, already chosen to die, and Guy took him through a veronica, almost losing his balance as he gritted against the pain in his leg. His cape flapped in the wind, and the young bull came back for a second charge. His legs were throbbing as he brought him close, executing the pass perfectly, but when the bull's shoulder nudged him, Guy sprawled, unable to keep his balance.

Very quickly, a caballero was in the ring, then another and they herded the young bull into the pen for slaughter animals.

"It will be better next time," Don San Benito said, walking beside Guy to the house. "Would you come here as my manager? You don't have to accept the *mano a mano,* you know. I don't care what they say, and neither does Vita. You can quit now, and you have a good future with the ganaderia."

"I haven't see Eduardo or Quiqui," Guy said.

"They left months ago for Spain," El Don shrugged, "Sometimes a man cannot do anything about what is happening around him, sometimes it is easier just to close one's eyes and pretend that something does not exist."

"The easy way is not always the right way," Guy said.

"Perhaps not for you," Don Benito said. "But, remember this, if you do not want to accept Tacon's challenge, there will be no disgrace in our eyes. It would make Vita happy."

"It is me, who would know the disgrace," Guy said.

"Close your eyes, matador," El Don advised, "The people will forget, and it will soon go away."

"Not in here," Guy tapped his chest. "I know I am not a coward, and I do not to want to be remembered as one. Perhaps it would be easier, if I were not American."

"It would indeed, matador," El Don conceded, "It certainly would. God bless you; you're going to need it."

His words were almost prophecy. It was as if Vita and he moved into separate worlds, and she kept away from him. Then, when she could stand it no more, she would rush into his arms and plead with him to give up the idea of the *mano a mano* with Tacon. "Who cares if you accept the challenge or not—not I!"

"I do, querida," he tousled her hair against his naked chest and kissed her ear. "I care for us. It is important."

"Can't it wait until you are well?" she pleaded, lifting her face to look in his eyes. "It would be a fair fight then."

"I get better every day," he said, and felt her tremble in his arms. He loved her, God how he loved her! but she was a woman, and he could not expect her to understand that this was a matter of honor, a challenge more from Marge than from Tacon and if he ran now, he would be running the rest of his life.

He wanted to spend the rest of his life with Vita.

She seemed almost adjusted to the inevitability of the *mano a mano* by the time Marcos arrived. Two days later, the cuadrilla came and they got down to the serious business of the coming fight. Day after day, bull after bull, and finally it came to the killing.

Guy had been through many "moments of truth" with the bulls. This was his first moment of truth with himself. He took the sword and muleta, and began again the last act, the part where he had taken the bull's horn in his last fight.

Sweat broke out all over his body as he stood in front of the bull. Slowly, he draped the muleta to his right, then with almost imperceptible movement, his wrist snapped the muleta, drawing the bull's charge.

Guy knew just one way to kill, straight and honest.

It would have been easier to kill from the side, but he killed over the horns, just as he had always done, and when he finished, the caballeros and his cuadrilla were shouting.

He had killed again, and he was not a coward.

CHAPTER SIXTEEN

THE FIRST KILL WAS NOT the last at San Benito, there had to be many more before he was ready to face a bull in the ring. Marcos saw to it that the bull's sizes increased steadily, and El Don watched carefully, almost heedless that they were now using the good bulls.

Marcos had met with Tacon's manager, and the fight was scheduled in two weeks, at the Cinco de Mayo festival in Monterey. With this deadline, each day became more and more important, and each day found Guy wanting to go on in spite of his physical exhaustion.

The newspapers were flaunting the *mano a mano*, and Guy was beginning to feel the pressure of time. He watched the papers for the critics' columns, and hardly a day passed without some mention of the challenge.

It was three days before the fight that Guy found the article about scouts being there from Mexico City.

"We've got to fight another bull today," Guy told Marcos that afternoon.

"My matador," Marcos pleaded, "You are exhausted. You had better rest."

Guy wiped his face with a handkerchief, looked up at the stands where Vita sat next to Don San Benito, and signaled for another bull.

Just one more kill.

He was too tired, and the bull was just a little too quick, and Guy had to grab the horns to keep from being gored again. The cuadrilla and caballeros swarmed into the ring, and right behind them came Vita. Guy had fallen, his teeth and hands clenched. "No! God, no!"

His leg felt hot and warm, and blood oozed out staining his trousers to a dark, deep red.

The corona was open.

Guy actually cried as they carried him to the house, the doctor was summoned, and Vita waited with him in the bedroom. Guy was stretched on the bed; she had managed to stop the bleeding, and the doctor would sew it up. In the meantime, there was nothing to do but wait. Vita had held her feelings in check too long already, and the silence between them was strained.

"Don't just sit there," Guy looked at her, "Curse or something."

She sighed, "I can't curse you, you know that. Are you going to try to go on with this fight?"

"I have to fight Tacon," he said.

She turned exasperated, "You don't have to fight anyone! To Hell with Tacon! Papa has told you that you could come here and run this ranch; this is a rich ganaderia, and we need you —"

"Come to me, Vita," he lifted his hand.

"No," she looked away. "If I come over there, you'll kiss me and I won't say what I've got to say."

"What do you have to say?"

"Please, Amor," she took one step toward him, then stopped, "Please don't fight in Monterey, for me."

"Vita, you are asking the impossible."

"If you insist on fighting, Amor," she said quietly, but firmly, and it was as though she were tearing out part of herself, "then it is over between us."

And, she meant it.

Guy tried to make her see his point of view, but the only thing Vita understood was that the man she loved was going to face a bull in a senseless *mano a mano* with a novillero who could not hold a candle to his ability. For some strange mannish reason, it was more than just a fight, it was a matter of manhood itself, and she did not understand it. She did not care what the critics said, or the columnists or anyone else. Right now he was alive, and if he went into that ring disabled, he might come out dead.

He would fight; he did not have to tell her, she heard him talking to the doctor. They could deaden the pain, and bandage the corona in such a way that he could fight, and the pain would hardly be noticeable.

"Just so I can stand," Guy told the doctor.

"You are rushing things, matador," the doctor said, "but I understand."

They left San Benito on the fourth, with the fight scheduled for the next day, and Vita remained behind. She did not come to the car to see Guy off, and when he tried to see her, her door was closed.

Guy felt as if someone had tied a lead brick on each of his shoulders, as he left. He sank back in the car seat and let Marcos and El Don carry on the conversation, but even their forced talk withered in the mood that settled over them.

Guy was black, black. He felt black all over, and he wanted to twist his angry frustration out. Marge had set this up, urging Tacon to make the challenge, and now she was driving a wedge between him and Vita.

She did not want him, but she would not let him go. Guy felt the frustration worst of all, it was like facing a blankwall. He had to fight, and Vita could not see his way. It was fight, or fade out branded as a coward. This was his only challenge to a *mano a mano;* if he won it, as he knew he could, he could leave the bullring with honor, but if he ducked the fight, he could never hold his head up in bullfighting circles again.

Why couldn't she understand?

Of course, he understood about the way she felt, with him still suffering from the corona he took in Agua Caliente, but this was a matter of pride.

It simply had to be this way.

But, thinking about it did not help.

Neither did liquor, because he killed a bottle of Scotch and had sent for the second when there was a knock on his door, and Marge stood there.

"Hello, lover, how is the ailing torero?"

"As if you gave a tinker's dam." Guy started to slam the door, but she came in without an invitation.

"Be nice to your loving wife," she said. "Where is the virgin?"

"Wouldn't you like to know?" Guy had to bite his tongue to keep from lashing out at her. "For your information, there is nothing between us any more. I came here just to fight."

"You're alone, lover!" She exclaimed and came to him, "Now that is no way to be on the night before the big fight. I should know, I've been through hundreds of "night befores" with you. That's what a wife is for, right, lover?"

"Why don't you leave me alone?"

"Come here, darling," she moved in front of him, lifting her lips to be kissed. "There is a party just three doors down. It's going to be real nice; why don't you join us?"

"I'm sick of you."

"Kiss me!" she smiled, "That always makes it easier."

He lifted his right hand to his left shoulder, and the next sound in the room was the crack of his knuckles across her face. She fell back surprised, as he loomed over her, she wiped a streak of blood from her chin.

"I want you to understand something Marge," Guy spoke very clearly. "When this fight is over, we're getting a divorce.

I've asked you for a divorce many times, but it was not what you wanted. Well, now I'm going to divorce you. I'm going to play the game by your rules, and the law here is very easy. I don't ever want to see you again; now get out of my room."

She crouched before him, horrified that he talked to her this way. She was losing her meal ticket, "Guy, you don't mean what you're saying — think of the bad publicity."

"I'm sure you'll see to that," he said, "Now get out."

"Guy, I could be good to you," she said.

"I don't want anything you've got, ever again." He lifted his finger, pointing to the door, "O – u – t!"

When she was gone, he collapsed on the bed; then twisting, he buried his face in the pillows, and he shuddered, as he realized that there was nothing in his life, absolutely nothing. Vita was gone, and he had just thrown Marge out the door.

It was very lonely.

Even the second bottle of Scotch did not help, and he left the hotel. He walked and walked.

Monterey was a big town, and practically no one recognized him. It was over an hour later that he found the whorehouse section, and buxom dark girl leaned out a window and beckoned to him with her finger.

"Come jere, Yankee," her pronunciation was jarringly like Bambi, "I help you forget."

He started to turn back, but to what?

The steps were dirty and worn, and the inside of the house had a heavy hanging odor of cheap perfume, but her room was clean. She was already stripping as Guy came in "Five dollars American money, Yankee."

"Three."

"I settle for four," she smiled. "I work for nothing, maybe sometime. You look good."

She was just a whore, a lousy sweet-smelling whore, but it was a way to forget a sweet-smelling virgin. Her breasts were big and naked, with large rouged nipples, and she undulated against him, bouncing them against his chest. "Jou like Esperanza, Yankee man?"

"I like big breasts," he laughed, then patted her rear, "I like it hot back here."

"Oh Yankee!" she shrilled, "It's forever summer there."

And, as if to prove it, she hurried him through his own stripping, and then stretched on her sagging bed, spread-eagled.

He fell beside her, lying on his back, and then she noticed the huge bandage around his leg. "What is that, Yankee?"

"Don't you know a corona when you see it?" He tousled her black hair, and saw her eyes cloud.

"Who are jou?" She flipped on her belly, her breasts brushing the yellowish sheet. "I want no trouble with the police."

"You'll have no trouble with the police, Esperanza," he grinned. "I'm a bullfighter."

"Aiyee!" She slapped the side of her face, "El Oro!"

"Yes."

"What luck! It is good luck to have a bullfighter on the night before his fight! Jou can have it free." She nuzzled down beside him, earthy and plain; she wanted him and she was glad he was here. It was not beautiful, it was not artistic. It was sex. It was driving away the first approach of the fear, and knowing that his body would be able to react tomorrow. He fondled her breasts, cupping and squeezing them, but she did not need exciting, she was excited by him.

They found one another twice before he slept, then he woke and took her again before he left, and she followed him to the door, and the last he saw of her was one large breast peeping out at him as he reached the door, and went onto the street. He hailed a cab, and went back to the hotel. A shower, three drinks of Scotch and two cigarettes later, he was asleep.

It was troubled sleep, but sleep.

He could hear the noise of the party, and twice he heard knocking on his doors. The bastards, he thought, they did not have to face bulls tomorrow, they could drink and have sex and go on all night.

He felt like he was dying.

The mood was worse the next day, but there was one good sign. Paco had the red Suit of Lights. It was his lucky suit, and he liked to fight in it. Only today, it was more than luck; it was necessary to cover the possible blood stain. Red did a very good job of disguising the blood.

When he was completely dressed and ready, they left him alone. He went to *La Macarena*. "Just one more time *Macarena*, please don't let them kill me — don't let the bulls kill me today."

Marcos was brooding when he came out of the room; there was a small mob in the lobby, but the Monterey police were very effecting in clearing a way for Guy and his cuadrilla. Part of them were already at the ring, but Paco came with him, bringing his jeweled sword and heavy dress cape. Marcos smoked almost endlessly, and when they arrived at the ring behind a shrill police escort, Guy himself chain-smoked in the patio. Tacon was there, dressed beautifully in a new Suit of Lights, which Guy figured was bought with his money by Marge. She was absent, and he could guess that she would be cheering for his bulls today. Even if the bull won, she would lose nothing, and she knew it.

"Did she come?" he turned to Marcos.

"I don't know maestro, she said she would not," Marcos spoke of Vita, and saw Guy's eyes close, blinking against the sun.

"You truly love her, don't you maestro?"

"I did," he said.

"You do, maestro; maybe things will change."

Guy turned away as the alguaciles clattered into the patio leading their horses, all plumed and bedecked for the paseo. The alguacil wore a long black cape, with a wide black hat with a blood-red ostrich plume. He mounted, and beckoned to his second, who climbed into his saddle. They looked around; there were two minutes to go. The elder constable looked at his watch, checked with the younger and then signaled to the gatekeeper.

A wooden clacker brought the praying members of the cuadrilla to their feet, and they got in line. Guy gathered his dress cape under his left shoulder, straightened his montera, and nodded to the alguacil.

He lifted his hand, then dropped it; "Vamanos!"

The gates flew open, and Guy could hear the blare of brass trumpets pealing *La Macarena*. The alguaciles moved up on their horses, and the paseo began.

For a fleeting second, Guy glanced into the chapel, and suddenly everything changed.

Vita was with the bullfighters' women.

She looked deep into his eyes; neither of their lips moved, but in that second, both knew the other was in love. They loved each other, and now it would be a perfect day.

His bulls were big, black and fury on hooves, but they were good. They charged straight, and hooked clean. Guy worked them close, ignoring the cheers for Tacon, and giving his complete talent to the work at hand.

He brought the horns closer and closer, each time, never budging from his stance. He pulled their horns down with naturals, demanding and taking complete control of all three bulls. His kills were perfect, hilted deep and accurate and the bulls dropped in their tracks, and when it was over and the last bull was dead, the crowd stood up and cheered.

They pelted the ring with hats and pillows; bills floated in the evening air, and they waved wildly, forcing him through one, then two, then a third triumphant circle of the ring. He threw his montera into the stands and they filled it again and again with money, and waved white handkerchiefs at the judge.

First they awarded the ears, and the handkerchiefs fluttered thick and the cheers were like a rumbling roar filling the stand. The judge signaled for the tail to be given, and the crowd boomed its approval as he circled the ring with his awards.

They loved him, and they stood stamping their feet, clapping their hands and hundreds and hundreds of white handkerchiefs fluttered at the judge.

They gave him two hooves, and at last they let him leave the ring. She was waiting as he ran toward her, tears streaming down her cheeks.

"Matador! Amor! I love you," she kissed him again and again, "I don't care how it has to be, I need to be with you. I love you."

He circled her waist and led her toward the parked car. Marcos was there; the entire cuadrilla cheered as he passed, and no one, not even the defeated Tacon, noticed the torero's limp.

He winked at Marcos, "Do you think you'll like raising bulls?"

"Muy bien, maestro," he grinned widely, "How do you think you'll like rising sons?"

Guy glanced at Vita and smiled, "Muy bien, Marcos, that's exactly what I intend to do right away."

THE END